VAINGLORY

VAINGLORY

by

RONALD FIRBANK

ADELAIDE
MICHAEL WALMER
2013

Vainglory first published 1915
This edition published 2013

by

Michael Walmer
49 Second Street
Gawler South
South Australia 5118

ISBN 978-0-9873678-8-4 paperback
ISBN 978-0-9873678-9-1 ebook

VAINGLORY

I

"AND, then, oh yes! Atalanta is getting too pronounced." She spoke lightly, leaning back a little in her deep arm-chair. It was the end of a somewhat lively review.

On such a languid afternoon how hard it seemed to bear a cross! Pleasant to tilt it a little—lean it for an instant against somebody else. . . . Her listener waved her handkerchief expressively. She felt, just then, it was safer not to speak. Tactfully she rose.

On a dark canvas screen were grouped some inconceivably delicate Persian miniatures.

She bent towards them. "Oh, what gems!"

But Lady Georgia would not let her go.

"A mother's rôle," she said, "is apt to become a strain."

Mrs. Henedge turned towards her. "Well, what can you do, dear?" she inquired, and with a sigh she looked away sadly over the comparative country of the square.

Lady Georgia Blueharnis owned that house off Hill Street from whose curved iron balconies it would have seemed right for dames in staid silks to lean melodiously at certain moments of the day. In Grecian-Walpole times the house had been the scene of an embassy; but since then it had reflowered unexpectedly as a sympathetic background, suitable to shelter plain domesticity—or even more.

Not that Lady Georgia could be said to be domestic. . . . Her interests in life were far too scattered.

Known to the world as the Isabella d'Este of her day, her investigations of art had led her chiefly outside the family pale.

"It is better," Mrs. Henedge said, when she had admired the massive foliage in the square, and had sighed once or twice again, " to be pronounced than to be a bag of bones. And thank goodness Atalanta's not eccentric! Think of poor little Mr. Rienzi-Smith who lives in continual terror lest one day his wife may do something really strange—perhaps run down Piccadilly without a hat. . . . Take a shorter view of life, dear, don't look so far ahead! "

" I was thinking only of Monday."

" There will be eleven bridesmaids besides At'y! "

" They will look Satanic."

" Yes; it's perhaps too close to picture them! "

" I don't know, yet," Lady Georgia said, " what I shall wear. But I shall be very plain."

" The cake," Mrs. Henedge said, beginning to purr, " is to be an exact replica of the Victoria Memorial."

" Do you know where the honeymoon's to be spent? "

" They begin, I believe, by Brussels——"

" I can hardly imagine anyone," Lady Georgia observed, " setting out deliberately for Brussels."

" I suppose it does seem odd," Mrs. Henedge murmured, looking mysteriously about her.

The room in which she found herself was a somewhat *difficult* room. The woodwork by Pajou had been painted a dull, lustreless grey, whilst the curtains and the upholstery of the chairs were of a soft canary-coloured silk striped with blue. Here and there, in magnificent defiance, were set tubs of deep crimson and of brilliant pink azaleas. Above the mantelpiece was suspended a charming portrait of Lady Georgia by Renoir. No one ever warmed their hands there, or before the summer wilderness of plants, without exclaiming "How wonderful it is!" In this portrait she was seen promenading slowly in an economical landscape, whilst a single meagre tree held above her head its stiff branches lightly, screening her from the sun by its just sufficient leaves. On the opposite side of the room hung a second portrait of herself with her husband and her children—a lovely Holy Family, in the Venetian manner, and in between, all round the room, at varying heights, in blotches of rose and celestial blue, hung a sumptuous *Stations of the Cross*, by Tiepolo. Upon the ceiling, if one cared to look so high, some last few vestiges of the embassy might be seen—quivers, torches, roses, and all the paraphernalia of Love. . . . But the eyes, travelling over these many obstacles, would invariably return to the Venetian portrait, spoken of, as a rule, somewhat breathlessly as the *Madonna in the Osprey*.

Glancing from it to her hostess, Mrs. Henedge had not observed the remotest resemblance yet. She was waiting. . . . Except, she considered, for dear Lord Blueharnis, a fine, dashing St. Joseph, with blue, slightly bloodshot eyes, and the darling children, and the adorable Pekinese, it was decidedly a *Madeleine Lisante*. Striking, as it most unquestionably was, of Lady Georgia herself, it was not a satisfactory portrait. But how, it might pardonably be asked, was it likely to be? How was it possible for a painter to fix upon canvas anyone so elusive? He must interpret. He must paint her soul, taking care not to let her appear, as an inferior artist *might*, an overdressed capital sin.

Lady Georgia's face, indeed, was as sensitive as a calm sea to the passing clouds. She had variety. Often she managed to be really beautiful, and even in her plainest moments she was always interesting. Her nature, too, was as inconsistent as her face. At first sight, she was, perhaps, too individual to make any very definite impression. . . . A single pink flower

9

on her black frock, this afternoon, made her look, somehow, very far away.

Who can she be angling for, Mrs. Henedge wondered, and for whom is At'y becoming too pronounced? Was it for poor Lord Susan, who was sick, so everyone said, of the world at three-and-twenty?

At this notion she caressed, with a finger of a creamy glove, a small bronze of a bird with a broken wing.

Mrs. Henedge, the widow of that injudicious man the Bishop of Ashringford, was considered, by those who knew her, to be Sympathy itself. His lordship, rumour reported, had fallen in love with her at first sight one morning while officiating at a friend's cathedral, when she had put him in mind of a startled deer. She was really only appropriating a hymn-book, as she had afterwards explained. Their marriage had been called a romance. Towards the end, however, the Bishop had become too fe-fi-fo-fum-Jack-in-the-Beanstalk altogether. She had had a horrid time; but still, she was able to speak of him always as "*poor dear Leslie*," now that he was gone. To-day, perhaps, it might be said of her that she had deserted this century for—she had hardly settled which. Wrapped in what looked to be a piece of Beauvais tapestry, she suggested a rumble of chariots, a sacking of Troy. As Lady Georgia observed, quite perceptibly, she was on the brink of . . . Rome.

But reflections were put to flight, as some of the angels, from the famous *Madonna*, and several of the Pekinese came whirling into the room.

"It ran away in Berkeley Square."

"She had been having ices."

"On her head were two very tall green feathers."

"The policeman went away with her parasol."

"She was on her way to see us."

The children were very much excited. "Hush, darlings!" Lady Georgia exclaimed. "And when you're calmer, explain who it was that ran away from Berkeley Square."

"Grandmamma did!"

"Who would have thought," said Fräulein, appearing, "that a one-horse cab could do *so much mischief!*"

They were returning from the large heart of Bloomsbury, where the children were frequently taken to learn deportment from the Tanagras in the British Museum. After posing meaningly as a Corinthian, or practising sinking upon a camp-stool like an Athenian, they came home, as a rule, rampageous.

"This afternoon they are uncontrollable!" Fräulein murmured, attempting to hurry them away. But Mrs. Henedge, with an arm about a child, was beginning to expand.

"Her complexion," she observed, "is as lovely as ever; but she *begins to look older!*"

As a foreigner, Fräulein could fully savour the remark. She had succeeded, only lately, to Mademoiselle Saligny, who had been dismissed for calling Marie Antoinette a doll. Unfortunately, as Lady Georgia had since discovered, her Teutonic scepticism varied scarcely at all, from the Almighty to a can of hot water; but this was more pardonable, she considered, than labelling Marie Antoinette a doll. Distinguished, or harmless doubts were these!

"It's really rather an escape!" Lady Georgia murmured, as soon as they were gone; "my mother-in-law's dictatorialness is becoming so impossible, and in this warm weather she's sure to be out of sorts."

She stretched out a hand, listlessly, towards a red, colossal rose. So many talismans for happiness fettered her arms! She could hardly move but the jingling of some crystal ball, or the swaying of some malachite pig, reminded her of the fact that she was unhappy. "I can't bear," she said, "James to arrange the flowers, he *packs* them down into the vases." She got up and loosened some. " And when Charles does them," she murmured, " they're invariably swooning away! Come and see, though, all I've been doing; our lease, you know, doesn't expire until two thousand and one. And so it's quite worth while to make some little improvements! "

But Mrs. Henedge seemed disinclined to ſtir. Seated upon a sofa entirely without springs, that had, moſt likely, once been Juliet's bier, it appeared she had something to confide. Something was troubling her besides " *the poor Guards, in all this sun!* "

" My dear Georgia," she said, " now that you've told me your news, I want to tell you of a moſt exquisite discovery."

Lady Georgia opened wide-wide eyes. " Is it some new thing," she inquired, " about Mrs. Hanover? "

Mrs. Henedge looked about her. " It's rather a secret ſtill," she continued, " and although in many ways I should have liked to have told Ada, she would probably immediately tell Robert, and he, in confidence, would, of course, tell Jack, and Jack would tell *everybody*, and so——"

" Better say nothing to Ada! "

Mrs. Henedge heaved a sigh.

"Do you remember Professor Inglepin?" she asked. " His mother was a Miss Chancellor . . . Fanny. Well, quite lately, whilſt in Egypt, the Professor (he terrifies me! he's so thin, he's so fierce!) came upon an original fragment of Sappho. And I'm having a small party at my house, on Sunday, with his assiſtance, to make the line known."

Lady Georgia became immediately animated. The Isabella d'Eſte in her awoke.

" My dear, how heavenly! " she exclaimed.

" Exceptional people," Mrs. Henedge hinted nervously, " are coming."

" O—h? "

"Mrs. Asp, Miss Compostella, the Calvallys!"

"It will be delightful!"

"Well, you won't blame me, dear, will you, if you're bored?"

Lady Georgia closed her eyes. "Sappho!" she exclaimed. "I'm wondering what I shall wear. My instinct would dress me, I believe, in a crinoline, with a yellow cashmere shawl, and a tiny turquoise bonnet."

Mrs. Henedge became alarmed. "I hope we shall be all as *Ingres* as possible," she said, "since there's not much time to be Greek. And now that I've told you, I must fly! No, darling, I can't even stay to look at the improvements; since the house is yours for so long, I shall see them, perhaps, again. I'm going this evening with the Fitzlittles to the Russian dancers." And she added melodiously from the stairs: "I do so *adore* Nijinsky in *Le Spectre de la Rose*."

II

Mrs. Henedge lived in a small house with killing stairs just off Chesham Place.

" If I were to die here," she had often said, " they would never be able to twist the coffin outside my door; they would have to cremate me in my room." For such a cottage, the sitting-rooms, nevertheless, were astonishingly large. The drawing-room, for instance, was a complete surprise, in spite of its dimensions, being ocularly curtailed by a somewhat trying brocade of drooping lilac orchids on a yellow ground.

But to-day, to make as much space as possible to receive her guests, all the household heirlooms—a faded photograph of the Pope, a bust of *poor dear Leslie*, some most Oriental cushions, and a quantity of whimsies, had been carried away to the top of the house. Never before had she seen the room so bare, or so austere.

As her maid exclaimed: " It was like a church." If an entire Ode of Sappho's had been discovered instead of a single line she could have done no more.

In the centre of the room, a number of fragile gilt chairs had been waiting patiently all day to be placed, heedless, happily, of the lamentations of Thérèse, who, while rolling her eyes, kept exclaiming, " Such wild herds of chairs; such herds of wild chairs! "

In her arrangements Mrs. Henedge had disobeyed the Professor in everything.

Professor Inglepin had looked in during the week to ask that severity might be the key. " No flowers," he had begged, " or, at most, placed beside the fragment (which I shall bring), a handful, perhaps, of——"

"Of course," Mrs. Henedge had replied, "you can rely upon me." And now the house was full of rambler roses and of blue sweet-peas.

A buffet, too, had arisen altar-like in her own particular sanctum, an apology to those whom she was unable to dine; nor, for toothsome curiosities, had she scoured a pagan cookery-book in vain. . . .

Glancing over the dinner list whilst she dressed, it seemed to her that the names of her guests, in neat rotation, resembled the cast of a play. " A comedy, with possible dynamics! " she murmured as she went downstairs.

With a tiara well over her nose, and dressed in oyster satin and pearls, she wished that Sappho could have seen her then. . . . On entering the drawing-room she found her beautiful Mrs. Shamefoot as well as her radiant Lady Castleyard (pronounced Castleyud) had already arrived, and were entertaining lazily her Monsignor Parr.

" Cima's Madonnas are dull, dull, dull," Mrs. Shamefoot was saying, looking over the Monsignor's shoulder at her own reflection in the glass.

Mrs. Shamefoot, widely known as " Birdie," and labelled as politics, almost compels a tear. Over-shadowed by a clever husband, and by an exceedingly brilliant mother-in-law, all that was expected of her was to hold long branches of mimosa and eucalyptus leaves as though in a dream at meetings, and to be picturesque, and restful and mute. As might have been foreseen, she had developed into one of those decorative, self-entranced persons so valued by hostesses at dinner as an ideal full stop. Sufficiently self-centred, she could be relied upon to break up a line, or to divide, with grace, any awkward divergencies of thought. Her momentary caprice was to erect with Lady Castleyard, to whom she was devoted, a window in some cathedral to their memory, that should be a miracle of violet glass, after a design of Lanzini Niccolo.

It was therefore only natural that Lady Castleyard (whose hobby was watching sunlight through stained glass) should take the liveliest interest in the scheme —and through the mediation of Mrs. Henedge was hoping to kindle a window somewhere very soon.

A pretty woman, with magnificently bold shoulders and a tiny head, she was, as a rule, quite fearlessly made up. It was courageous of her, her hostess thought, to flaunt such carnationed cheeks. Only in a Reynolds or in a Romney did one expect to see *such a dab.*

" Tell me! Tell me! " she exclaimed airily, taking hold of Mrs. Henedge. " I feel I must hear the line before everyone else."

Mrs. Henedge, who did not know it, pressed to her lips her fan.

" Patience! " she murmured, with her subtlest smile.

Monsignor Parr gazed at her with heavy opaque eyes.

Something between a butterfly and a misanthrope, he was temperamental, when not otherwise . . . employed.

" I must confess," he observed, " that Sappho's love affairs fail to stir me."

" Ah, for shame! " Mrs. Henedge scolded, turning from him to welcome an elaborate young man, who, in some bewildering way of his own, seemed to find charming the fashions of 1860.

" Drecoll? " she inquired.

" Vienna," he nodded.

" This is Mr. Harvester," she said. She had nearly said " Poor Mr. Harvester," for she could not endure his wife.

Claud Harvester was usually considered charming. He had gone about here and there, tinting his personality after the fashion of a Venetian glass. Certainly he had wandered. . . . He had been into Arcadia, even, a place where artificial temperaments so seldom get—their nearest approach being, perhaps, a matinée of *The Winter's Tale*. Many, indeed, thought him interesting. He had groped so. . . . In the end he began to suspect that what he had been seeking for all along was the theatre. He had discovered the truth in writing plays. In style—he was often called obscure, although, in reality, he was as charming as the top of an apple-tree above a wall. As a novelist he was almost successful. His books were watched for . . . but without impatience.

" Cleopatra," he said, " was so disappointed she couldn't come."

" I thought I saw some straw——"

" Miss Compostella," the servant tunefully announced.

"Ah, Julia! "

A lady whose face looked worn and withered through love, wearing a black gauze gown, looped like a figure from the Primavera, made her way mistily into the room.

Nobody would have guessed Miss Compostella to be an actress; she was so private-looking. . . . Excessively pale, without any regularity at all of feature, her face was animated chiefly by her long red lips; more startling even than those of Cecilia Zen Tron, *cette adorable Aspasie de la décadence Vénitienne*. But somehow one felt that all Miss Compostella's soul was in her nose. It was her one delicate feature: it aspired.

" How was I? " she murmured, when she had shaken hands. " I was *too nervous* for words! "

" You were completely splendid."

" My dear, how beautifully you died! "

Miss Compostella was experimenting, just then,

at her own theatre, with some tableaux inspired from Holbein's *Dance of Death*.

"Two persons only," she said, "were present at my matinée. Poor things! I asked them back to tea. . . . One of them is coming here to-night."

"Really! who can it be?"

"He plays the piano," she said, "composes, and he has the most bewitching hair. His name is Winsome Brookes."

Mrs. Shamefoot tittered.

"Oh, Winsome's wonderful," Mrs. Henedge exclaimed. "I enjoy his music so much. There's an unrest in it all that I like. Sometimes he reaches to a pitch of life. . . ."

"His tired ecstasy," Claud Harvester conceded, "decidedly is disquieting."

Miss Compostella looked at him. She admired terrifically his charming little leer; it was like a crack, she thought, across the face of an idol. Otherwise, she was afraid, his features were cut too clearly to make any very lasting appeal. . . .

Nevertheless, for her general calm she could have wished that it had been next year.

Each day she felt their position was becoming more strained and absurd. She had followed Claud Harvester closely in his work, until at length she stood beside him on a pinnacle at some distance from the ground. And there they were! And she was getting bored. It disgusted her, however, to be obliged to climb down, to have had her walk for nothing, as it were.

With a smile that might, perhaps, have been called pathetic, she turned towards her hostess, who, with a deeply religious eye upon Monsignor Parr, was defending her favourite Winsome Brookes from Mrs. Shamefoot's innuendoes.

"But why, why, *why*," she inquired, "do you think him dreadful?"

" Because I think he's odious," she replied.

" Children irritate you, dear, I know, but he will do great things yet! "

" Can one ever say? "

" The moſt unexpeᶜted thing in my life," Monsignor Parr broke in gently, " was when a certain cab-horse from Euſton ran away! "

" Thanks for your belief in us," Mrs. Henedge exclaimed gratefully, rising to greet an indolent-looking woman who brought with her, somehow, into the room, the tranquillity of gardens.

Mrs. Calvally, the wife of that perfeᶜt painter, was what her hoſtess called a complete woman. She was fair, with dark Tzigane eyes, which, slightly dilated, usually looked mildly amazed. Like some of Rubens' women, you felt at once her affinity to pearls. Equanimity radiated from her leisurely person. She never became alarmed, as her friends well knew, even when her husband spoke of going away and leaving her to live alone in some small and exquisite Capitol.

She would juſt smile at him sensibly, pretending not to hear. . . . Secretly, perhaps, his descriptions of places intereſted her. She would have missed hearing about the White Villa, with its cyprus-tree, between the Opera House and the Cathedral, and she let him talk about it like a child. She did not mind when the town chosen was Athens, which was near Malta, where she had a cousin, but she had a horror of Buchareſt.

George Chriſtian Calvally accompanied his wife, unhappy, perhaps, at playing, if even for only a few hours, an oboe to her violin. His face was delicate and full of dreams. It was a perfeᶜt *grief face.*

" My dear Mary," Mrs. Henedge exclaimed affeᶜtionately, leading the sympathetic woman to the moſt sylvan seat she could find, a small settee, covered with a chintz all Eve's apples, and a wonderful winding snake, " had you to be very ſtrategic? "

19

" Oh, not at all," Mrs. Calvally replied; " but what do you think followed us into the house? "

Mrs. Henedge looked alarmed.

" Oh, nothing so dreadful. . . . Only a butterfly! "

Mrs. Shamefoot, who was listening, became positively ecstatic.

How nice it was to escape, if even for a second, from the tiresome political doings of which she was so tired. Not that she could always catch everything that was said, now that she wore her hair imitated from a statue of the fifth century. . . .

But the inclusion to-night, however, of Winsome Brookes was something of a trial. Without any positive reason for disliking him, she found him, perhaps, too similar in temperament to herself to be altogether pleased.

He came into the room a few minutes later in his habitual dreamy way, as might one upon a beauty tour in Wales—a pleasant picture of health and . . . inexperience. From the over-elaboration of his dress he suggested sometimes, as he did to-night, a St. Sebastian with too many arrows.

A gentle buzz of voices filled the room.

Mrs. Henedge, admirable now, was orchestrating fearlessly her guests.

Mr. Sophax, a critic, who had lately lost his wife and was looking suitably subdued, was complimenting, just sufficiently, a lady with sallow cheeks and an amorous weary eye. This was Mrs. Steeple.

One burning afternoon in July, with the thermometer at 90, the ridiculous woman had played *Rosmersholm* in Camberwell. Nobody had seen her do it, but it was conceivable that she had been very fine.

" Tell me," she said to Mr. Sophax, " who is the Victorian man talking to that gorgeous thing—in the gold trailing skirts? "

"You mean Claud Harvester. His play the other night was a disaster. Did you see it?"

"It was delightfully slight, I thought."

"A disaster!"

"Somehow, I like his work, it's so lightly managed."

"Never mind, Mr. Harvester" Lady Georgia was saying to him, "I'm sure your play was exquisite; or it would have had a longer run."

He smiled.

"How satirical you are!"

She was looking tired, and not a bit wonderful; it was one of her lesser nights.

"I wish she would give her poor emeralds a rest," a lady like a very thin camel was observing to Monsignor Parr.

A flattering silence greeted the Professor.

"I'm afraid you must feel exhausted from your field day at the British Museum," Mrs. Henedge said to him half hysterically, as they went downstairs.

The success of the dinner-table, however, restored her nerve. To create a slight atmosphere she had made a circuit of the table earlier in the evening, scattering violets indiscriminately into the glasses and over the plates.

For a moment her guests forgot to chatter of themselves. They remembered Sappho.

The Lesbian wine (from Samos. Procured, perhaps, in Pall Mall) produced a hush.

Claud Harvester bethought him then that he had spent a Saturday-to-Monday once, in Mitylene, at "a funny little broken-down hotel upon the seashore."

It had been in the spring, he said.

"In the spring the violets in Athens are wonderful, are they not?" Mrs. Calvally inquired.

"Indeed, yes."

She spoke to him of Greece, but all he could

remember of Corinth, for instance, was the many
drowned lambs he had seen lying upon the beach.

"*Ah! Don't speak to me of Corinth!*"

"What a pity—and in Tanagra, tell me, what did
you see?"

"In Tanagra . . .?" he said, "there was a kitten
sunning himself in the Museum, beside a pile of broken
earthenware—handles of amphoræ, arms and legs of
figurines, and an old man seated in the doorway
mending a jar."

"How extraordinary!" she marvelled, removing
with extreme precaution an atom of cork that had
fallen into her glass. "Really! Is that all?"

"Really all," he murmured, looking with sudden
interest at Miss Compostella, whose face, *vis-à-vis*, he
thought, still bore traces of his comedy.

He could appreciate her subtle mask quite enor-
mously just then: now that she recalled to him his
play. How very delightful she was!

"Surely," he reflected, "her hair must be wired?"

Probably, as his wife had hinted once, her secret
lay simply in her untidiness. She had made it a study.
Disorder, with her, had become a fine art. A loose
strand of hair . . . the helpless angle of a hat. . . .
And then, to add emphasis, there were always quantities
of tiny buttons in absurd places on her frocks that
cried aloud, or screamed, or gently prayed, to be
fastened, and which, somehow, gave her an air of
irresponsibility, which, for simple folk, was possibly
quite fascinating.

"She's such a messy woman," Cleopatra had said.
"And, my dear . . . so unnatural! I wonder you
write plays for her. If I were a man, I should want
only . . ."

And she had named the impossible.

"I feel I want to go away somewhere and be ugly
quietly for a week," Miss Compostella was confiding

to George Calvally, as she cut a little wild-duck with her luminous hands. "The effort of having to look more or less like one's photographs is becoming such a strain."

He sympathised with her. "But I suppose," he said, "you are terribly tied."

"Yes, but you know, I love it! Next month I'm hoping to get Eysoldt over to play with me in Maeterlinck. . . . It isn't settled, there's some incertitude still, but it's almost sure!"

"Her Joyzelle!" he began to rave.

"And my Selysette!" she reminded him.

"Now that Maeterlinck is getting like Claud Harvester," the Professor, without tact, put in, "I don't read him any more. But at all events," he added graciously, "I hope you'll make a hit."

"A hit! Oh, I've never done anything so dreadful," she answered, turning her attention towards her hostess who, beneath her well-tipped tiara, was comparing the prose of a professional saint to a blind alley.

"But what does it matter," Lady Georgia inquired, leaning towards her, "if he has a charming style?"

In the vivacious discussion that ensued Mrs. Steeple, imprudently, perhaps, disclosed to Winsome Brookes her opinion of Miss Compostella.

"Oh, Julia's so stiff," she said, "she will hold herself, even in the most rousing plays, as though she were Agrippina with the ashes of Germanicus, and in depicting agony she certainly relies too much upon the colour of her gown. Her Hamlet," and she began to laugh, "her Hamlet was irresistible!"

And Mrs. Steeple laughed and laughed.

Her laughter, indeed, was so hilarious that Winsome became embarrassed.

"Her H-H-Hamlet was irresistible!" she repeated.

"Do tell us what is amusing you!" Miss Compostella inquired.

But Mrs. Steeple appeared to be too convulsed.

"What has Winsome been saying?" her hostess wished to know.

In none of these disturbances did Mrs. Shamefoot care to join. Mentally, perhaps, she was already three parts glass. So intense was her desire to set up a commemorative window to herself that, when it was erected, she believed she must leave behind in it, for ever, a little ghost. And should this be so, then what joy to be pierced each morning with light; her body flooded through and through by the sun, or in the evening to glow with a harvest of dark colours, deepening into untold sadness with the night. . . . What ecstasy! It was the Egyptian sighing for his pyramid, of course.

As might be feared, she appeared this evening entirely self-entranced. Indeed, all that she vouchsafed to her neighbour, Mr. Sophax, during dinner, was that the King had once been "perfect to her" in Scotland, and that she was fond of Yeats.

"If you cannot sleep," she said to him, "you've only to repeat to yourself *Innisfree* several times. You might be glad to remember. . . ."

As Mrs. Henedge had explained, it was only a fragile little dinner. She was obliged to return to the drawing-room again as soon as possible to receive her later guests. It occurred to her as she trailed away with the ladies that after the Professor's Sapphic postscript they might, perhaps, arrange some music. It would bring the evening to a harmonious close.

There was Winsome, fortunately, to be relied upon, and Mrs. Shamefoot, who sang the song of Thaïs to her mirror very beautifully, and later, she hoped, there would be Mrs. Rienzi-Smith, who composed little things that were all nerves . . . and who, herself, was so very delightful. . . .

In the drawing-room she was glad to find that

wonderful woman, Mrs. Asp, the authoress of *The Home Life of Lucretia Borgia*, refreshing herself with coffee and biscuits while *talking servants* to Mrs. Thumbler, the wife of the architect, and the restorer of Ashringford Cathedral.

" She was four years with Lady Appledore," Mrs. Asp was telling her, taking a bite at her biscuit, " and *two* at the Italian Embassy, and although one wouldn't perhaps, think it, I must say she was always scrupulously clean."

" My dear Rose," Mrs. Henedge said, sailing up, " I do hope you haven't been here long? " She seemed concerned.

" I—I—I, oh no! " Mrs. Asp purred in her comfortable voice, using those same inflections which had startled, so shockingly, the Princess H. of B. when, by telephone, she had confessed: " Yes . . . I am Mrs. Asp. . . . We're getting up a little bazaar and we expect you royalties to help! "

" And there, I believe, is Mira? " Mrs. Henedge said, turning towards a young girl who, seated in a corner, seemed to be counting the veins in her arms.

" I admired your valsing, the other night," she said to her, "at the de Lerens'. It's so brave of you, I think, to like dancing best alone."

Mira Thumbler was a mediæval-looking little thing, with peculiar pale ways, like a creature escaped through the border of violets and wild strawberries of a tapestry panel.

As a rule nobody ever noticed her (in spite of a few eccentricities, such as dancing singly at parties, etc., sufficiently manifest, possibly, to have excited attention). She was waiting to be found. Some day, perhaps, a poet or a painter would come along, and lift her up, high up, into the sun like a beautiful figurine, and she would become the fashion for a while . . . set the New Beauty.

" These apparent icebergs," Mrs. Henedge thought, as she touched Mira's charming and sensitive hand, " one knows what they are! "

" My dear, what a witty frock! " Lady Georgia said to her, fingering it. " Is it that little Miss Finch? It's a perfect psalm! "

" The cupids are imitated from a church frieze," Mira explained, holding out the stiff Italian stuff of ruby and blue woven with gold.

" I have seldom seen anything so splendidly hard! " Lady Castleyard admired. " You're like an angel in a summer landscape, reposing by the side of a well! " And holding her coffee-cup at an angle, she surveyed the room, a bored magnificence.

" There's no plot," Mrs. Asp, who seemed utterly unable for continuity, was confiding to a charmed few, " no plot exactly. It's about two women who live all alone."

" You mean that they live just by themselves? "

Mrs. Thumbler was unable to imagine a novel without a plot, and two women who lived so quietly! . . . She was afraid that poor dear Rose was becoming dull.

" I wonder you don't collaborate! " she said.

" Oh no. . . . Unless I were in love with a man, and *just as a pretext*, I should never dream of collaborating with anybody."

" You would need a sort of male Beatrice, I suppose? "

" How amusing it would be to collaborate with Mr. Harvester," Mrs. Steeple murmured, glancing towards Miss Compostella, who just then was looking completely flattered, as she closed her eyes, smiled, and lifted, slightly, a hand.

" Certainly I adore his work," Mrs. Asp admitted. " He pounces down on those mysterious half-things . . . and sometimes he fixes them! "

26

" Do you know Mr. Harvester? " Mira asked.

" Of course I know Mr. Harvester. . . . He scoured Cairo for me once years ago, to find me a lotus. Why?"

" I should so much like to meet him."

" My dear, what an extraordinary caprice! " Mrs. Henedge exclaimed, disengaging herself to receive a dowager of probable consequence, who, in spite of a crucifix and some celestial lace, possessed a certain poetry of her own, as might, for instance, a faded bacchante. It needed scarcely any imagination at all to picture her issuing at night from her cave on Mount Parnassos to watch the stars, or, with greater convenience, perhaps, strutting like the most perfect peacock, before some country house, over the rose-pale gravel; as charming as the *little stones* in the foreground of the Parnassos of Mantegna.

Lady Listless, or Atossa, as her friends respectfully called her, had the look of a person who had discovered something she ought not to know. This was probably brought about by being aware of most people's family feuds, or by putting merely two and two together. In the year her mistakes came to thousands, but she never seemed to mind.

" I've just been dining with the Barrows," she said solemnly to Mrs. Henedge, keeping her by the hand. " Poor little Mrs. Barrow has heard the Raven. . . . She came up hurriedly last night from the country and has taken refuge at the Ritz Hotel."

" It's hardly likely to follow her, I suppose? " Mrs. Henedge inquired anxiously.

" I don't know, I'm sure. The hotel, it appears, already is particularly full. . . . The last time, you remember, they heard it croak, it was for old Sir Philidor." And looking exceedingly stately, she trailed away to repeat to Mrs. Shamefoot her news: " Violet has heard the Raven! "

" To be painted once and for all by my husband

27

is much better than to be always getting photo-graphed! " Mrs. Calvally was saying to a Goddess as the Professor came in.

" I know," the Goddess answered; " some of his portraits are really *très Velasquez*, and they never remind you of Whistler."

" Oh, beware of Mr. Calvally! " murmured Mrs. Asp, flitting past to seize a chair. " He made poor Lady Georgia into a greyhound, and turned old General Montgomery into a ram—he twisted the hair into horns."

An unwarrantable rush for places, however, announced that the critical moment had come.

" Well, darling," Mrs. Thumbler, triumphant, explained to her daughter, excusing herself for a sharp little skirmish with Monsignor Parr, " I was scarcely going to have him on my knee! " And with emotion she fluttered a somewhat frantic fan.

" I think your *young musician* so handsome," Mrs. Asp whispered to Mrs. Henedge, giving a few deft touches to a bandeau and some audacious violet paste. " With a little trouble, really, he could look quite Greek."

" Is your serial in *The Star*, my dear Rose, ever to be discontinued? " Mr. Sophax, who stood close behind her, stooped to inquire.

" Don't question me," she replied, without turning round. " I make it a rule never to be interviewed at night."

Next her, Lady Listless, perched uncomfortably on Claud Harvester's *New Poems*, sat eyeing the Professor with her most complacent smile. She knew hardly anything of Sappho, except that her brother, she believed, had been a wine merchant—which, in those times, was probably even better than being a brewer.

" But if they had meant to murder me," the camel-

28

lady was mysteriously murmuring to Monsignor Parr, " they would not have put chocolate in the luncheon-basket; my courage returned to me at that!" when a marvellous hiss from Mrs. Asp stimulated Miss Compostella to expand.

" My dear, *when an angel* like Sabine Watson . . ." she was heard to exclaim vaguely above everyone else.

Julia, just then, was in high feather. George Calvally had promised to design for her a beautiful poster, by the time that Eysoldt should arrive, with cyprus-trees and handfuls of stars. . . .

But the Professor was becoming impatient.

It would be utterly disgusting, Mrs. Henedge reflected, if he should get desperate and retire. It was *like* Julia to expatiate at such a time upon the heavenliness of Sabine Watson, who was only *one*, it seemed, of quite a troop of angels.

To conceal her misgivings she waved a sultry yellow fan. There was a forest painted upon it of Arden, in indigo, in violet, in sapphire, in turquoise, and in common blue. The fan, by Conder, was known perversely as *The Pink Woods.*

" I'm not going to inflict upon you a speech," the Professor said, breaking in like a piccolo to Miss Compostella's harp.

" Hear, hear! " Mr. Sophax approved.

" You have heard, of course, how, while surveying the ruins of Crocodileopolis Arsinoë, my donkey having——"

And then, after what may have become an anguishing obbligato, the Professor declaimed impressively the imperishable line.

" Oh, delicious! " Lady Listless exclaimed, looking quite perplexed. " Very charming indeed! "

" Will anyone tell me what it means,"Mrs.Thumbler queried, " in plain English? Unfortunately, my Greek——"

"In Plain English," the Professor said, with some reluctance, "it means: 'Could not' [he wagged a finger] 'Could not, for the fury of her feet!' "

"Do you mean she ran away?"

"Apparently!"

"O-h!" Mrs. Thumbler seemed inclined to faint.

The Professor riveted her with his curious nut-coloured eyes.

"Could not . . ." she murmured helplessly, as though clinging to an alpenstock, and not quite sure of her guide. Below her, so to speak, were the roof-tops, pots and pans: Chamonix twinkling in the snow.

"But no doubt there is a *sous-entendu?* " Monsignor Parr suspiciously inquired.

"Indeed, no!" the Professor answered. "It is probable, indeed, that Sappho did not even mean to be caustic! Here is an adventurous line, separated (alas!) from its full context. Decorative, useless, as you will; a water-colour on silk!"

"Just such a Sapphic piece," Mrs. Asp observed, with authority, "just such a Sapphic piece as the *And down I set the cushion*, or the Γέλως παιδοφιλώτερος, or again the *Foolish woman, pride not thyself on a ring.*"

"I don't know why," Lady Georgia confessed, "it thrills me, but it does!"

"Do you suppose she refers to——"

"Nothing of the kind!" the Professor interrupted. "As Mrs. Asp explains, we have, at most, a broken piece, a rarity of phrase . . . as the poet's *With Golden Ankles*, for instance, or *Vines trailed on lofty poles*, or *With water dripped the napkin*, or *Scythian Wood* . . . or the (I fear me, spurious) *Carrying long rods, capped with the Pods of Poppies.*"

"And isn't there just one little tiny wee word of hers which says: *A tortoise-shell?* " Mrs. Calvally murmured, fingering the huge winged pin in the back of her hair.

" I should say that Sappho's powers were decidedly
in declension when she wrote the Professor's ' water-
colour,' " Mrs. Steeple said disparagingly.
" I'm sure I don't see why! "
" Do you remember the divine Ode to Aphrodite?"
she asked, and rapidly, occult, archaic, before anybody
could stop her, she began to declaim:

" Zeus-begotten, weaver of arts deceitful,
From thy throne of various hues behold me,
Queen immortal, spare me relentless anguish;
Spare, I beseech thee.

Hither haste, if ever of old my sighing
Moved thy soul, O Goddess, awhile to hear me,
From thy Father's house to repair with golden
Chariot harnessed.

Lovely birds fleet-winged from Olympus holy
Fluttering multitudinous o'er the darksome
Breast of Earth their heavenly mistress hastened
Through the mid ether;

Soon they brought the beautiful Aphrodite;
Softly beamed celestial eyes upon me;
And I heard her ask with a smile my trouble,
Wherefore I called her.

What of all things most may appease thy frenzy?
Whom (she said) would Sappho beguile to love her?
Whom by suasion bring to heart adoring?
Who hath aggrieved her?

Whoso flies thee, soon shall he turn to woo thee;
Who receives no gifts shall anon bestow them;
If he love not, soon shall he love, tho' Sappho
Turneth against him!

—Lady now too come, to allay my torment;
All my soul desireth, I prithee grant me;
Be thyself my champion and my helper,
    Lovely Dione! "

" Exquisite, dear; thanks."

" Christianity, no doubt," the Professor observed, with some ferocity, to Monsignor Parr, " has invented many admirable things, but it has destroyed more than it has created! " The old pagan in him was moved.

" You have been stirring our antenatal memories, Mrs. Steeple," Claud Harvester said.

" Have I? " she laughed.

" Mr. Brookes has promised to play to us," Mrs. Henedge said hurriedly, with sufficient presence of mind.

" Can he play *Après Midi sous les Pins* ? " the camel-lady wondered.

" Certainly," Winsome snapped, lifting from the piano a photograph of two terrified-looking little boys, which somehow had been forgotten. " I can play anything when I have the music! "

" Poor Mr. Calvally . . . he looks always so atrociously sad! " Lady Listless murmured, staring about her.

" It's unfortunate," Mrs. Rienzi-Smith said to her, " that the Professor seems so displeased."

" Well, what more could he want? We were all on footstools before him."

" What am I to play to you? " Winsome asked of Mrs. Henedge. " A fanfare? A requiem? "

" Oh, play us something of your own. Play your ' Oakapple,' from *The Suite in Green*."

But, " to break the ice," as he put it, he preferred the exciting *Capriccio Espagnol* of Rimsky-Korsakoff to anything of his own.

32

" But didn't you hate waiting for Othello to press the pillow? " Lady Castleyard was questioning Miss Compostella. " I should have got up and screamed or rung the bell, I'm sure I should! "

" Really? I think it's almost the only moment in the play that gives an actress an opportunity to see where are her friends," Julia replied.

" Just as I've observed," Mira Thumbler murmured maliciously to Claud Harvester, " that a person who begins by playing the Prelude of Rachmaninoff seldom plays anything else——"

" Oh no," he said. " When Winsome plays like that, I want to live in a land where there'd be eternal summer."

Mira looked amused.

"All places, really," she said, " have glamour solely in essence, didn't you know, like a drop of scent! "

She paused a moment to listen to her neighbour. " So appallingly badly kept," the Goddess was describing Valhalla. " In the throne-room, for instance, the candles leaning in all directions . . . and everything else the same! "

" Tell me," Mira said, turning towards Claud Harvester abruptly, and speaking with sudden passion, " why are you so *genial* with everyone? Why? It's such—a pity! "

" Good heavens," he exclaimed, startled, " what is the matter? "

But she had moved away.

" No, something of your own." Mrs. Asp was begging Winsome, rather imprudently.

" I will play through the first act of my *Justinian*, if you think it wouldn't be too long."

" A few of the leading themes, perhaps," Mrs. Henedge suggested.

" Very well. I will begin with the folk-song of the Paralytics."

" That will be delightful."

" You must imagine them," Winsome explained to Lady Listless, who was sitting next to the piano, " grouped invalidishly about the great doorway of Santa Sophia. The libretto directions will say that there is a heavy violet moon, and that it is a warm June night."

Whilst listening to music Lady Listless would allow her aspirations to pass unrestrainedly across her face. They passed now, like a flight of birds.

" And here," Winsome murmured airily, without ceasing, and playing with delightful crispness of touch, " is the *pas* of the Barefooted Nuns."

Lady Listless became rhapsodical. " It's almost as delicious," she breathed, " as the Sugar-Plum Fairies' Dance from *Casse Noisette*."

Mrs. Asp also nodded her approbation. " The finale was distinctly curious," she exclaimed. " Just like the falling of a silver tray! "

" And this," Winsome explained, folding his arms and drooping back shyly, " is the motive for Theodora."

" My dear young man," Lady Listless objected, " but I hear nothing . . . nothing at all."

" The orchestra ceases. There's audible only the movement of her dress——"

And, suddenly irresponsible, he began to play " Summer Palace—Tea at Therapia," which seemed to break away quite naturally into an exciting Czardas of Liszt.

" But how amusing! "

Mrs. Henedge, slightly anxious now, judged that the moment had come to ask Mrs. Shamefoot to sing. Winsome was hardly serious. It was perhaps a pity, she reflected, though it couldn't be helped, that her dear Mrs. Shamefoot cared only for the extremely exalted music of the modern French school. Just then, *a dose of Brahms,* she felt, would have done them all more good, but doubtless Mrs. Rienzi might be relied upon to bring the evening to a calmer close with some of her drowsy gipsy dances.

" And when she died she left everything for the Capuchin Fathers," Mrs. Shamefoot was telling Monsignor Parr as Mrs. Henedge approached.

" Sing, dear . . .? " she said. " Oh, I don't really know if I can. . . . The room is so hot. And there are so many roses! I don't know which look the redder, ourselves or the roses. And I have been chatting all the evening. And my voice is just the least bit tired. But if you simply insist, and Dirce will play my accompaniment; and if——"

And ultimately, as was to be hoped, she rose and fluttered over the many prayer rugs to the piano.

Seldom, George Calvally thought, watching her, had he seen a more captivating creature.

" Do you think her as graceful as she passes for? " He could hear Winsome Brookes inquire.

" Graceful? " the camel-lady answered. " No, really! She's like a sack of coals."

" Ah! je suis fatiguée à mourir! " Mrs. Shamefoot sang. " Tous ces hommes ne sont qu'indifférence et brutalité. Les femmes sont méchantes et les heures pesantes! J'ai l'âme vide. . . . Où trouver le repos? . . . Et comment fixer le bonheur! O mon miroir fidèle, rassure-moi; dis-moi que je suis toujours belle, que je serai belle éternellement; que rien ne flétrira les roses de mes lévres, que rien ne ternira l'or pur de mes cheveux; dis-moi que je suis belle, et que je serai belle éternellement! éternellement!

" Ah! tais-toi, voix impitoyable! voix qui me dis: ' Thaïs ne serai plus Thaïs! . . . Non, je n'y puis croire; et s'il n'est point pour garder la beauté de secrets souverains, de pratiques magiques, toi, Vénus, réponds-moi de son éternité! Vénus, invisible et

présente! ' . . . Vénus, enchantement de l'ombre!
réponds-moi! Dis-moi que je suis belle, et que je serai
belle éternellement! Que rien ne flétrira les roses de
mes lèvres, que rien ne ternira l'or pur de mes cheveux;
dis-moi que je suis belle et que je serai belle éternellement! éternellement! éternellement! "
    " Exquisite, dear; thanks! "
    " Oh, she's heavenly! "
    " Edwina never sang so! "
    " If she becomes invocatory again," Mrs. Asp
whispered, beating applause with a finger upon a fan,
" I shall have my doze—like Brunhilde."
    " You would be most uncomf'y," Mr. Sophax
observed, " and then who would finish your serial
for *The Star*. . . . No one else could."
    It was too true. . . . Nobody else could draw an
unadulterated villain with the same nicety as Mrs.
Asp. How she would dab on her colours, and then
with what relish would she unmask her man; her
high spirits during the process were remarked by all
her friends.
    But there was to be another song, it seemed, for
with her back to the room and a glow of light flooding
her perfectly whitened shoulders, it was unlikely that
Lady Castleyard would yield immediately to Mrs.
Rienzi her chair. With her head slightly inclined, it
was permitted to admire the enchanting fold of her
neck and the luxuriant bundles of silvered hair wound
loosely about her head, from whence there flew an
aigrette like a puff of steam.
    " An aigrette," Mrs. Asp calculated, " at least six-
teen inches long! " No; there would be at least two
more songs, she felt sure.
    " They tell me," she said to Mr. Sophax, shaking
long tearful earrings at him, " that the concert at
Jarlington House, the other night, was a complete
success, and that Lady Castleyard played so well that

someone in the audience climbed over a great many poor toes and tried to kiss her hands. . . . Atossa says that he received quite a large cheque to do it! "

But a troublesome valse, that smouldered and smouldered, and flickered and smouldered, until it broke into a flame, before leaping into something else, and which was perhaps the French way of saying that " still waters run deep," cast for an instant its spell, and when it was over Mrs. Henedge decided that she would ask Mira Thumbler to dance.

Not unlikely it would be giving an old maid her chance. Indeed, at seventeen, the wicked mite was far too retiring. Nobody ever noticed her. So many people had said so! And her poor mother with nothing but daughters; her only child a girl. . . .

She found Mira lolling beneath a capacious lamp-shade looking inexpressibly bored. Her hostess gathered by her silhouette that the temptation to poke a finger through a Chinese vellum screen, painted with water-lilies and fantastic swooping birds, was almost *more* than she could endure.

" My dear, won't you dance for us? " she asked.

Mira looked up.

" Oh, forgive me, please," she exclaimed, " but I should feel far too like . . . *you know!* "

She smiled charmingly. . . .

" The daughter of Herodias? " Mrs. Henedge said. " Nonsense! Don't be shy."

" Anything you might ask for . . ." George Calvally murmured kindly, who was standing near.

" Do you mean that? "

" Of course I mean it! "

She considered his offer.

" Then," she said, " I'm going to sit to you for my portrait. Oh, it's stupid and dull of me, I suppose, to have so few features—just a plain nose, two eyes, and a mouth—still! " She flung a hand up into the

37

air to be admired. She smiled. She looked quite pretty.

"I shall be immensely flattered," the painter said.

And so—after what seemed almost incredible adjustments—Mira danced.

On their way home he spoke of her lovely Byzantine feet.

Mrs. Calvally yawned. "It's extraordinary that a little skimped thing like Miss Thumbler should fascinate you!" she said.

III

Just at the beginning of Sloane Street, under the name of Monna Vanna, Mrs. Shamefoot kept a shop.

It was her happiness to slap, delicately, at monotony by selling flowers.

Oh, the relief of running away, now and then, from her clever husband, or from the fatiguing brilliance of her mother-in-law, to sit in the mystery of her own back parlour, with the interesting Dina or with Jordan, her boy!

She found in this by-life a mode of expression, too, for which her nature craved. It amused her to arrange marvellous sheaves of flowers to perish in the window before a stolid public eye; and some of her discords in colour were extremely curious. Often she would signal to her friends by her flowers, and when, for some reason, at the last Birthday Mr. Shamefoot had been carefully overlooked, in a freakish mood she had decked the window entirely with black iris.

But notwithstanding politics, it was declared that in all England nobody could wire Neapolitan violets more skilfully than she.

It was her triumph.

In a whole loose bouquet she would allow a single violet, perhaps, to skim above the rest—so lightly!

On her walls hung charming flower studies by Fantin Latour, and by Nicholson, intermingled with some graceful efforts of her own—impressions, mostly, of roses; in which it might be observed that she made always a great point of the thorns. And when there was nobody much in town these furnished the shop.

This morning, however, Mrs. Shamefoot sat down

to make a wreath—she hardly knew for whom; but since to-day was only Monday, she had a presentiment that one might be needed. . . .

With her dark eyes full of soul she commanded Dina to fetch her one. She fancied she might make ready a lyre, with some orchids and pink lilies, and numberless streaming ribands; something suitable for a disappointed débutante, and hardly had she commenced her work when Mrs. Henedge came into the shop.

" My dear Birdie, who ever expected to see you! " she exclaimed. " I thought you fluttered in only now and then, to see how everything was getting on——"

She seemed embarrassed.

Mrs. Henedge had looked in early indeed solely to implore Dina to persuade her mistress to take back some of the rambler-roses from her last night's party, but now, as she put it, they were face-to-face her heart *failed* her.

" What is the cost of those catkins? " she inquired, pointing, in her agitation, at something very fabulous-looking indeed.

They might go, she reflected, to Winsome Brookes. Often she would thank him for music by a cake or a small shrub, and Rumpelmeyer's to-day was not in her direction.

Mrs. Shamefoot became vaguely flurried.

" I don't know, dear, " she replied. " When I try to do arithmetic clouds come down upon me like they do in *Tannhäuser*."

With a gasp, Dina crossed over to a book—she seemed to be suffering still from lack of breath. The pretty creature lived in a settlement *William Morris*, some paradise on the confines of the Tube, from whence she would appear breathless each morning, and would stay so, usually, until the Guards went by. When this occurred she would commence her duties by flying to the window to sprinkle water from a Dresden can over the grateful flowers, admiring, meantime, the charms of the cavalcade through the handle of one of Mrs. Shamefoot's psychological baskets, or whatever else might be in stock.

After this, she would calm down slightly for the day. But unfortunately, even so, Dina lacked sense. Even in the afternoon she would say: " The roses this morning are two shillings each."

" I did so enjoy last night," Mrs. Shamefoot said to Mrs. Henedge, " though, when I got back, for no reason . . . Soco simply stormed at me; but I was splendidly cool. I said nothing. I just *looked* at him."

" You poor darling," Mrs. Henedge said sympathetically: " What an unhappy life! "

In silence Mrs. Shamefoot stuck a lily in her lyre.

"It is sometimes," she said, "rather unpleasant. . . ." She began suddenly to cry.

" They are not catkins at all," Dina observed, apparently herself somewhat surprised. " They're orchids."

But Mrs. Henedge ignored her. She was determined to have nothing to do with them.

" There," she exclaimed, " went poor little Scantilla stalking along. Did you notice her? She had on a black jacket and a vermilion-magenta skirt——"

" Half-mourning! "

" Exactly."

" I dare say she's off to the wedding," Mrs. Shamefoot said. " Lady Georgia and At'y are coming in, I believe, on their way. The wedding is at Holy Trinity."

Mrs. Henedge looked out at the stream of carriages through the flowers. The seldom coarse or unspiritual faces of the passing crowd . . . veiled by plum-blossom, had an effect, she thought, of Chinese embroidery.

" I can't quite forgive Nils for getting married,"

Mrs. Shamefoot murmured, twirling in the air a pale rose with almost crimson leaves. " I used to like to talk nonsense with him. He talked agreeable nonsense better than anyone I ever knew."

" I'm more concerned for Isolde," Mrs. Henedge said. " I pity her, poor child, married to a charming little vain fickle thing like that! "

" Oh, what does it matter? " Mrs. Shamefoot queried. " When I took Soco I married him for certain qualities which now, alas! I see he can have never had."

" That's just what's so sad! I mean, I'm afraid you did something commonplace after all."

Mrs. Shamefoot became discomposed.

" Oh, well! " she said, " when I got engaged I was unconscious, or very nearly. I had fallen sound asleep, I remember, off an iron chair in the park. The next day he had put it in the paper; and we none of us could raise the guinea to contradict . . ."

" Have you sent Isolde the——? "

" No, . . ." Mrs. Shamefoot confessed.

To nine brides out of ten she would make the same gift—a small piece of Italian gauze.

When the recipient, holding it to the light, would catch a glimpse of her fiancé through it, she began to realise something of its significance.

" What did you send? " Mrs. Henedge wondered.

A tenth bride invariably was interesting.

" I sent her," Mrs. Shamefoot said, " a Flemish crucifix, with ruby nails for the hands and feet. . . ."

" Dear Biddy. . . . I ran only to a pack of cards; supposed once to have belonged to Deirdre. I got them in Chelsea."

But Dina at the telephone was becoming distressing.

" Hullo! Yes! No! To whom am I speaking? "

The " To whom am I speaking? " characterised, as a rule, her manner.

"An order," she said, "for a shower of puff-puffs for Mrs. Hanover, to be at Curzon Street to-morrow morning by nine o'clock. If the flowers are not delivered by then she will expect them at the Law Courts."

"Poor thing!" Mrs. Shamefoot murmured; "send her a lovely spray, and tell Jordan to be there by eight."

Jordan lately had been imported from the country, only to exclaim, the first time it rained: "It's too-wet-for-to-go-far!"

It had been very disheartening.

Mrs. Shamefoot considered her lyre; in its way, it was going to be as wonderful as the anchor of peonies she had made for the late Lord Mayor.

"Do you remember it, dear?" she said, beginning to laugh. "It was so *huge*, so perfectly huge, that it had to be tilted sideways to get it out of the shop."

But Mrs. Henedge was considering an amazingly elegant landaulette—a landaulette that seemed to her to positively whistle with smartness.

"Here comes Lady Georgia, now," she exclaimed, "and Mrs. Mountjulian, 'Emily' is with her——"

"Oh, she's getting sinister and *passée*."

"Perhaps; but only sometimes! It's not so long ago that she was tinting her toes with blackberries to be a nymph! You'd never credit it, dear, but we were the same age once!"

"I shall hide behind the counter," Mrs. Shamefoot said, "if she comes in."

"For the love of heaven, mind the lyre!" Mrs. Henedge screamed as Mrs. Mountjulian entered.

Mrs. Mountjulian was long and slender, like an Imari vase, with a pretty, lingering manner which many thought tiresome.

As Miss Emma Harris the world had found her distinctly aloof. As the Duchess of Overcares, how-ever, she had been very simple indeed; it had been a new form, perhaps, of pride. And now, as Mrs. Mount-julian, she was becoming " aloof " again. To add a dash of picturesqueness to her career, her husband, it was said, was doing his utmost to get rid of her; and although she had been in an aeroplane disaster, a fatal gala performance, two railway accidents and a ship-wreck, she always came back—smiling.

" We've come to rifle you of your nicest flowers," Mrs. Mountjulian said.

" Oh, I need nothing," Atalanta explained. " Only to smooth my hair."

In a muslin frock with a broad blue sash, and a bridesmaid's bouquet of honeysuckle and meadow-sweet, she was looking engagingly pronounced. She needed only a mop and a pail to be altogether delightful.

" Isn't she *voyou?* " Lady Georgia said nervously. " I'm really afraid to be seen with her."

" My dear, you look a dove! " Mrs. Henedge murmured.

" Properly managed, nothing need ever clash," Mrs. Mountjulian assured Dina, singling out for herself a savage, multicoloured leaf.

But Lady Georgia appeared transfixed.

" For whom," she asked, " is that heavenly lyre? "

" ' For Time sleeps not, but ever passes like the wind . . .' " Mrs. Shamefoot replied vaguely.

" St. Catherine! "

" To the Queen of . . . Naples."

They smiled.

" Oh, do choose," Atalanta said, glueing down her hair inventively, with a perfect sense of style. " There's sure to be a struggle at the church. And Isolde will have a *crise des nerfs* or something if we aren't there soon. Besides, Victoria's getting impatient: I can see her dangling a long leg from the car into the street."

" It was too bad really of Mrs. Fox foisting her on to us," Lady Georgia said. " Prevent her, do, from getting out."

She was looking, perhaps, annoyed, in arsenic green with a hat full of wan white flowers.

" Blueharnis insists that you come to us for the Ashringford races," she said to Mrs. Shamefoot, as she said good-bye, " and stay at Stockingham for as long as you can."

" How sweet you are! If only to lie in the garden, I'll come."

" At present I'm revolving a Tragic Garden," Lady Georgia told her, " with cypress-trees, and flights of stairs."

" I'm admiring your pictures," Mrs. Mountjulian said, dawdling. " Those clouds—so stationary—surely are Cézanne? and the Monticelli . . .! And that alluring Nicholson. . . . Only last night I was talking to Sir Valerian Hanway; you know whom I mean? And he said: . . . ' It's an anxiety for a poor man to own beautiful things. Where would be the pleasure of possessing a Velasquez, and having to hold a pocket handkerchief all the time to the roof to keep out the rain?' "

" If she thought to embarrass me," Mrs. Shamefoot said as soon as they were gone, " I'm afraid she failed!"

" Poor woman! " Mrs. Henedge considered it diplomatic to say. " Either she is growing old, or her maid is getting clumsy. . . ."

"I should imagine both," Mrs. Shamefoot observed, returning to her lyre.

" I'm delighted, at any rate, that we shall see something of each other in Ashringford! We must contrive to conquer all difficulties to obtain the window."

" Otherwise," Mrs. Shamefoot said, " I shall try Overcares! "

" It's not so *obvious*, of course! "

" And the Bishop, I know, is not unfavourably disposed. . . . But somehow, dear, a manufacturing town is *not* the same."

" Indeed it isn't! "

" Besides, there were so many sickening stipulations——"

" The Bishop of Overcares is the most paralysing man I know," Mrs. Henedge said, " and she . . . Mrs. Whooper——"

" A terror! "

" A perfect terror! "

" Well, it's so nice of you to help me."

" And might a tiny nosegay be left for Mr. Brookes? Lilies he likes. . . . Just five or six; I'm making, unavoidably, in the opposite direction, or I'd drop them on his doorstep myself."

Mrs. Shamefoot stood a moment pensively watching Dina remove the dark hearts that stained from Winsome's lilies before continuing her wreath.

It would be quite too extravagant, she feared, when finished, for the penniless young man for whom her débutante had died. He could never afford to buy it.

What should be done?

Remove a few of the orchids? No!

Allow the father it? Certainly not.

Die and use it herself? Soco was so dilatory. . . .

She remained dreaming.

" Be so good," she called to Dina presently, " as to fetch me the scissors."

And, shaking her head sadly under her heavy hat, she cut a string to the lyre.

I V

13 SILVERY PLACE was the address of Mrs. Henedge's latest genius.

"A young boy," it was her custom to describe him.

With a few simple words she could usually create an interest.

The young boy, gentle reader, was Winsome Brookes.

Standing at his window, hairbrush in hand, we find him humming some bars of *Cimarosa*, whilst staring up at a far-off Fuji of clouds. The attitude was essentially characteristic. When not exercising those talents of his, Winsome Brookes would spend whole hours together grooming fitfully his hair.

"Don't mind me," his gracious lady often said to ·him, " if you care to calm your hair. I know that with you it takes the place of a cigarette." And at Chesham Place, sometimes, she would supply the needful weapons.

Just now, however, with two invitations for the same afternoon, he was looking pestered. . . .

"Will you not make, Andrew, that appalling noise?" he murmured distractedly, without turning round. "You make me shudder."

"It's extraordinary," Andrew answered briskly, waving, as he spoke, a file, " but ever since that Arabian ball, the paint clings to my finger-tips, as if to the cornice of a temple! "

Winsome removed an eye from the street.

"Well, need you point at me like a finger-post? " he irritably inquired.

47

" I consider your friend to be half a minion, and half an intellectual," Mrs. Henedge, who had never taken to Andrew in the least, had said once to Winsome Brookes. " That violet muffler, and the no collar . . ." was the official reason, but in reality, a lurid sketch of herself leaning upon the arm of an Archbishop of Canterbury whilst smiling across her shoulder into the eyes of Monsignor Parr accounted for the antipathy. She had come upon the trifle altogether suddenly at the Grafton Gallery and had decided at first it must be a Forain.

" I wish your breakfast would come," Andrew exclaimed disinterestedly, stretching himself out upon the floor—a *nature morte*.

" And so do I," Winsome complained. " But what is one to do? I order an egg, I wait an hour for it, and in the end most probably they'll bring me some fearful thing that looks like an auk's."

" A hawk's? "

" Oh, my dear friend. . . . An auk's. The great auk! " Winsome rolled his eyes.

Let us follow these bright ornaments.

The rooms of their occupants are sometimes interesting.

Taking for granted the large, unwieldly furniture, the mournful carpet, the low-spirited draperies, the brown paper of the walls, the frieze, in which Windsor Castle appeared again, and again, and again, and which a patriotic landlady (a woman like a faded Giotto) would not consent to hide lest it might seem to be disloyal, let us confine our observations to the book, the candlestick, the hour-glass, or the skull.

In a litter upon the mantelpiece—some concert fixtures, a caricature of Owen Nares, an early photograph of Andrew in a surplice, a sketch of Mildenberg as Clytemnestra, an impression of Felia Litvinne in Tristan, might be seen, whilst immediately above,

48

usually quite awry, was suspended a passionate engraving of two very thin figures wandering before a retreating sea.

Winsome, indeed, to Andrew's amusement, cared only for quite independent landscapes of disquieting colour. He found beauty in those long, ſtraight roads bounded by telegraph poles, between which some market cart would trundle through the pale midday.

Upon the piano, swathed in a scintillating shawl, rose up a modern figurine with a weary geſture, which, upon examination, was not lacking in signs that the original muſt almoſt certainly have possessed the proverbial kind heart of a black sheep. Beside it, againſt a ſtack of music, was propped a mask of Beethoven in imitation bronze, which, during the more ſtrenuous efforts of the player, would invariably slip, giving, often, the signal for applause.

While in a corner, intriguing the eye, reposed a quantity of boards: polished yellow planks, the planks of Winsome's coffin. These, in the event of a party, could be coaxed to extend the dinner-table. " If you're going to be ten for supper to-night," his landlady would say, " you'll need your coffin boards ſtretched out."

But as much as he was able Winsome sauntered out to dine.

In her cooking, he found his landlady scarcely solicitous enough about his figure. . . . So manifeſt, of course, at concerts. In her supremeſt flights the good woman would seldom get beyond suet. And even this was in her moſt Debussyish vein. . . . And the queſtion of concerts was occupying largely his thoughts juſt now.

Continually he was turning over in his mind the advisability of being re-baptised, this time—Rose de Tivoli. For musical purposes it sounded so much more promising, he considered, than Winsome Brookes. . . .

49   D

Two persons would come to hear Rose, whereas only one, and perhaps not even one . . .

But if Winsome Brookes had talent, Rose de Tivoli had genius!

Could he possibly be Rose?

Mrs. Henedge was inclined to think so. She had been, indeed, most hopeful:

" I'll take the Aeolian Hall, one afternoon," she had said, " and you can give the concert——"

To be—or not to be Rose! It was one of the things that was troubling him most.

" Ah! here comes breakfast now," Andrew observed, as Mrs. Henedge's floral gift was ushered in upon a tray.

> " ' I offer ye these violets,
>   Lilies and lesser pets,
>   These roses here pell-mell—
>   These red and splendid roses,
>   Buds which to-day uncloses,
>   These *orchids dear* as well.' "

" ' These opening pinks as well,' " Winsome corrected. And returning impassively to the window, he leaned out.

Everywhere, between the houses, those old and dingy houses, whose windows would catch the sunrise with untold splendour, showed plots of garden, like snatches of song. Sometimes of a summer morning, leaning from his window, it would not have astonished him greatly to have surprised the Simonetta of Boccaccio at the end of the shady place leaping lightly, with uplifted arms, between the trees, pursued by Guido degli Anastagi and his pack of hounds. . . . Nor were visions all. Across the street the Artistic Theatre, a brilliantly frescoed, Asian-looking affair, aspired publicly heavenwards every day. It was the adornment and the scandal of the place. Too late, now, to protest about the frescoes; they were there!

Winsome sighed. At that moment his gracious lady bored him badly.

For just as the bee has a finer nature than the wasp, so had Andrew the advantage of Winsome Brookes.

By nature mercenary, and, perhaps, a trifle mean, a handful of flowers suggested to him nothing very exactly. . . .

> " The courtyard clock had numbered seven
> When first I came; but when eleven
> Struck on my ears, as mute I sate,
> It sounded like the knell of Fate."

Winsome turned.

Nothing diverted Andrew more than to investigate Winsome's books.

With a *Beauty and the Beast* he was almost happy.

The entrance, fortunately, of breakfast put an end to the recitation.

Whilst Winsome breakfasted Andrew indulged himself by venting his indignation on Miss Compostella's poster for the *Dance of Death* at the theatre over the way.

" It's enough to make me cart the Magdalen back home! " he exclaimed.

" Perhaps some day," Winsome said, " I may go for curiosity to New York, but until then——! "

For Andrew frequently would model strange, unusual figures that were ostensibly Church pieces had they been more subdued . . . His Mary Magdalen, for instance, might be seen in the foyer of the Artistic Theatre, where, even there, it was usually abused. . . .

" The Eros looks at least sixty! " he observed, criticising the poster. " And Death in that small toque's absurd. Surely Death required a terrific Lewis and a Romney hoop to conceal the scythe."

" But Death isn't a woman! " Winsome objected, cracking the top of his egg.

" Indeed? Death is very often a bore."

" Only for Adonis," Winsome murmured absently.

" . . . Do I disturb you? "

" No, come in. Not in the least! "

" I thought," Andrew said coldly to the intruder, " that you went to the Slade! "

" Certainly; but not to-day! I shall run round later on, I dare say, for lunch at the British Mu-z. . . ."

" How fascinating! "

" I want you to come upstairs," the young man said plaintively to Winsome, " and tell me what Titian would have done. . . ."

" Me? " Winsome said.

" Yes, do come."

" Knowing you," said Andrew, " I should say that most likely he would have given her a richer background, and a more expensive silk."

" How can I," the young man queried, as he withdrew, " when the model has only a glove? "

" Why will you appal him? " Winsome asked; " he has the soul of a shepherd."

" Impossible."

" What are you saying? "

" Nothing; but when I look at your landlady's frieze," Andrew said limply, " I've a sort of Dickensey feeling coming on. I get depressed, I——"

Winsome swallowed his coffee.

" Then let's go."

" Il tend à leurs baisers la plume de sa main," Andrew began to warble inconsequently as he escaped downstairs.

V

"I WONDER you aren't ashamed, Sumph," Miss Compostella said to her maid, "to draw the blind up every morning on such a grey sky."

"Shall I draw it down again, miss?"

"Yes, please do. No, please don't. Come back to me again when I ring."

"And the shampoo?"

After the final performance of any play it was the maid's duty to perform this office to precipitate from the mind a discarded part.

"Washing-out-Desdemona," Sumph called it, dating the ceremony from then.

"It's hardly necessary," Julia said, "after such a light part. And, candidly, I don't quite agree with this romance-exhorting haste. For five whole weeks now, I'm only myself."

"Lord, may it keep fine," prayed the maid, lowering an inch the blind.

She was as stolid a mortal, it is probable, as ever graced a bedside or breathed at heaven a prayer.

"A light part," she said, "becomes a load during fever. And none of us are so strong as my poor——"

"But after Hermione," Julia objected, "I remained a week. . . ."

"After Hermione," the woman replied, "you could have gone ten days. After Hermione," she repeated loftily, "you could do as you pleased."

Sumph, indeed, worshipped Shakespeare. . . . Stratford, it appeared, was her "old home." Consequently, she was scarcely able to endure her mistress to appear in those pieces—pamphlets, or plays of

53

domestic persecution—in which all that could be done was to waft, with one's temperament, little puffs of rarefied air, now and again, across the footlights.

And yet it must be said that Sumph was a bad critic. It was just in these parts that her mistress most excelled.

Julia sat up and smiled.

Round the bed in which we surprise her hung a severe blue veil suspended from oblong wooden rings. Above it, a china angel upon a wire was suspended to complete the picture.

At the sight of her tired mistress set in bolsters the devoted woman was almost moved to tears.

" Oh, be quiet," Julia exclaimed. " I know exactly . . . I remind you of Mrs. So-and-so in some death scene. . . ."

Sumph straightened her cap, a voluminous affair drawn together in front in a bewildering bow.

" You do," she said, " miss. Of Mrs. Paraguay, or la Taxeira, as she was to become. She achieved fame in *Agrippina at Baiae*, in a single night. Never will I forget her pale face or her white crinoline. She was marvellous. It was that first success, perhaps, that drove her to play only invalid parts. Ah, miss, how lovely she looked with the treasures of half the Indies in her hair. . . ."

" Indeed? " Julia observed. " You're hurting my feet."

The woman turned away from anything so brittle.

" Tell me truthfully," Julia queried, " how am I looking? "

" Beautifully weary, miss."

Miss Compostella sank back.

Like some indignant Europa she saw herself being carried away by the years.

" Sumph," she said feebly, " what do you think of Mr. Harvester? "

" As a poet, miss, or as a man? "

54

" . . . As a poet."

" His poems are very cold and careful, miss; just what one would expect."

Julia turned her face to the wall.

Since her mother's death, caused, no doubt, by a flitting forth with an excursion ticket to Florence (Mrs. Compostella had succumbed almost immediately in the train), Julia had taken a charming house for herself in Sacred Gardens. The address alone, she hoped, would be a sufficient protection, and so spare her the irksomeness of a chaperon. And here, somewhat erratically, she lived with the invaluable Sumph, whom she ill-treated, and of whom, in her way, she was fond.

" Mr. Harvester came round last night, miss, just after you had gone," Sumph said; " and I'll confess to you I flew at him. At the totally unexpected, as they say, it's oneself that speaks."

" Indeed, it ought not to be."

" Surrounded as we are," said Sumph, " it's best to be discreet."

" I'm afraid you were very rude to him! "

" Oh, miss, why waste words on a married man? I'd sooner save my breath and live an extra day."

" Are you so *fond* of life? " Miss Compostella painfully inquired, her face turned still towards the wall.

" And an old gentleman, with the wickedest eye, called also, and asked if you was in."

" Did he give no name? "

" He left no card, but he called himself a saint," Sumph answered slyly.

Mr. Garsaint's political satire, *The Leg of Chicken*, which was to be played in Byzantine costume, was to be given at the Artistic Theatre in the autumn; unless, indeed, Miss Compostella changed her plans, and produced *Titus Andronicus*, or *Marino Faliero*, or a

55

wildly imprudent version of the *Curious Impertinent* at the last moment, instead. For if there was one thing that she preferred to a complete success, it was a real fiasco. And Mr. Garsaint's comedy would probably be a success! What British audience would be able to withstand the middle act, in which a couple of chaises-longues, drawn up like passing carriages, silhouetted the footlights from whence the Empress Irene Doukas (a wonderful study of Mrs. A.) and Anna Comnena lay and smoked cigarettes and argued together—at ease? And even should Mr. Garsaint's dainty, fastidious prose pass unadmired, the world must bow to the costumes, foreshadowing as they did the modes of the next century.

" How tiresome to have missed him! " Miss Compostella exclaimed, sitting up, and blinking a little at the light.

In the window hung a wicker cage of uncertain shape that held a stuffed canary. It had had a note sweeter than Chenal's once. . . . And there it was! Poor, sad thing!

" Angel! Sweet! Pet! Pretty! " Julia would sometimes say to it by mistake.

Through the vigilant bars of the cage she could admire a distant view of a cold stone church by Vanbrugh. The austere and heavy tower, however, did not depress her. On the contrary, she approved its solidity. Flushed at sunset, it suggested quite forcibly a middle-aged bachelor with possessions at Coutts. At times she could almost think of it as *James*. . . .

" And there are several hundred more letters waiting for you in the next room, miss," Sumph said.

To Julia's inquiry for a man with ecstasy to stage-manage, she had received several thousand applications.

" Go to the next room," Miss Compostella directed, " and choose me two with your eyes shut."

It was in the "next room" that Miss Compostella sometimes studied her parts . . . though for modern comedy rôles she usually went "upstairs."

She sank back now and waited.

With five weeks at her disposal, with the exception of a complaisant visit to Stockingham for a race party, it was her intention to lie absolutely still, preferably at a short distance from London, and explore her heart.

For indeed the dread of Miss Compostella's life was that she had not got one. Unless that sorrowful, soft, vague, yearning, aching, melting, kite-like, soaring emotion was a heart?

Could that be a heart?

From the mantelpiece came a sudden "whirr" from an unconcerned Sèvres shepherdess, a coquettish silence, followed by the florid chiming of a clock.

Noon; or very nearly—for as an object submits meekly to its surroundings, Julia's timepiece, invariably, was a little in advance.

She held out long arms, driftingly.

It was noon! Sultry noon—somewhere in the world. In Cintra now . . .

She lay back impassively at the sound of Sumph's Olympian tread.

A gesture might revive a ghost.

It was irritating to discover that one recalled Polly Whatmore in *The Vicar's Vengeance*, or Mrs. Giltspur in *The Lady of the Lake*.

The indispensable woman, holding the testimonials of the men of ecstasy, approached the bed.

" And Mr. Harvester is here, miss," she said sedately, lifting up her eyes towards the quivering angel. " Should I show him into the next room, or shall I take him *upstairs?* "

Julia reflected.

" No," she murmured; " put him in the dining-room and shut the door."

57

" Yes, miss."

" And, Sumph . . . offer him a liqueur, and something to read—of his own."

" Yes, miss."

" And, Sumph . . . I shall be getting up now in about half an hour."

She waited—and recast her arms expressively.

" Claud . . .? "

But the worst of it was, she reflected, that with a chair upon Mount Parnassos (half-way up) he was somewhat inclined to *dictate*. . . .

VI

To Ashringford from Euston is really quite a journey.

Only an inconvenient morning train, or a dissipated evening one—described in time-tables as the Cathedral Express—ever attempt at concentration. Normal middle-day persons disliking these extremes must get out at Totterdown and wait.

As a stimulus to introspection, detention cannot be ignored.

Cardinal Pringle, in his Autobiography, confesses that the hour spent on Totterdown platform, seated in deep despondence upon his trunk, came as the turning-point in his career.

Introspection, however, is not to be enforced.

" It will hardly take us until five o'clock, Violet," Mrs. Shamefoot observed to her old crony, Mrs. Barrow of Dawn, fumbling, as she spoke, with a basket, " to drink a small bottle of champagne. Is there nothing particular here to see? "

She looked out at the world, through a veil open as a fishing-net, mysteriously.

Where were the *sunburned sicklemen of August weary!* The *ryestraw hats!* Surely not many yards off.

Mrs. Barrow put up her sunshade.

" Oh yes," she said, " a cousin of Oliver Cromwell is buried not far from here; and in the same graveyard there's also the vault of a Cabinet Minister who died only the other day."

Mrs. Shamefoot produced with perfect sympathy a microscopic affair.

" In this heat," she observed, " champagne is so much more refreshing than tea."

Mrs. Barrow accepted with gratitude.

It may be remembered from some exclamations of Lady Listless that just lately she had "heard the Raven." It was said, however, about Dawn, that whenever she wished to escape to town for a theatre or to shop she would manage to hear its croak.

" I do hope," she exclaimed, " that Sartorious won't be at Ashringford to meet me; it's perfectly possible that he may."

" Well, there's no good in singing a dirge over what can't be helped; the connection's gone."

" What tactless things trains are!"

Mrs. Shamefoot shook a panoply of feathers.

" What is that curious watch-tower," she asked diplomatically, " between the trees?"

Mrs. Barrow began to unbend.

Life, after all, seemed less raw after a glass of champagne.

" I don't know, dear," she said, " but I think the scenery's so perfectly French."

" Isn't there a hospital near here—for torn hearts, where love-sick persons can stay together in quarantine to enjoy their despair and help each other to forget?"

" I don't know, dear," Mrs. Barrow said again, " but I believe there's a sanatorium for nervous complaints. . . . All the country round Totterdown belongs to Lord Brassknocker."

" Oh, he's dreadful!"

" And she's such a thorough cat."

" And poor Lord Susan!"

" Poor, *poor* Lord Susan."

" I can almost feel Ashringford Cathedral here," Mrs. Shamefoot remarked. "Aren't the hedges like the little low curtains of a rood-screen?"

" Exactly!"

" And aren't the——"

"My dear, what a dreadful amount of etceteras you appear to bring," Mrs. Barrow replied with some aridity.

Mrs. Shamefoot's principal portmanteau was a rose-coloured chest, which, with its many foreign labels, exhaled an atmosphere of positive scandal. No nice maid would stand beside it.

A number of sagacious smaller cases clambered about it now into frantic streets, and sunny open piazzas, like a small town clustering about the walls of some lawless temple.

Mrs. Barrow was appalled at so much luggage. She had been to the ends of the earth, it seemed, with only a basket.

Mrs. Shamefoot re-helped herself to Clicquot.

She was looking to-day incomparably well, draped in a sort of sheet *a la* Puvis de Chavanne, with a large, lonely hat suggestive of *der Wanderer*.

"The relief," she exclaimed, "of getting somewhere where clothes don't matter!"

"But surely to obtain a window in the Cathedral *they will*. You'll need an old Ascot frock, shan't you, for the Bishop?"

"Violet, I'm shocked! Can such trifles count?"

"Well, I dare say, dear, they help to persuade."

"Bishop Pantry is quite unlike Bishop Henedge, isn't he?"

"Oh, quite. The present man's a scholar! Those round shoulders. He will probably die in his library by rolling off the final seat of his portable steps."

"But not just yet!"

"You have read his *Inner Garden!*"

"Oh yes. . . . And *Even-tide*, and *Night Thoughts*, and the sequel, *Beams*. But they're so hard. How can it be good for the soul to sleep upon the floor, although it mayn't be bad for the spine."

"Besides, to tread the spiral path means usually a

61

bother . . ." Mrs. Barrow observed. " There are the servants! And to get a girl to stay in Ashringford——"

Mrs. Shamefoot fixed her eyes upon the hills that slid back, she thought, with a fine monastic roll.

" And is he very plain? " she asked.

" I should never say so. It's a fine Neronian head."

" Lady Anne is charming, isn't she? "

Mrs. Barrow hesitated.

" Sartorious," she replied, " thinks her wily."

" But she is charming? "

" Oh, well," Mrs. Barrow said evasively, " she doesn't shine perhaps at the Palace like dear Mrs. Henedge. I suppose we shall never replace *her* again! Fortunately, however, she's devoted to Ashringford and comes there nearly every summer. Since she's taken the Closed House she's thrown out fourteen bow-windows."

Mrs. Shamefoot snapped the lid of her basket.

" Who are these condottieri? " she inquired, as an imperious party drove up with considerable clatter.

Mrs. Barrow turned.

" Don't look more than you can help, dear," she exclaimed, in a voice that would have piqued a stronger character than Mrs. Lott, " it's the Pontypools."

" Ashringford people? "

" Theoretically."

Mrs. Shamefoot smiled.

" Sartorious——" Mrs. Barrow began.

" Thinks them? "

" Totally dreadful. They're probably reconnoitring. Mrs. Pontypool is usually spinning a web for some-one."

" The dowager's very handsome," Mrs. Shamefoot remarked, " in a reckless sort of way, but the girl's a fairy! "

" Oh, don't swear! Don't, don't swear! " Mrs. Pontypool was adjuring a member of her family, with brio, stepping, as she spoke, right into Mrs. Barrow's arms.

" Is it quite true," she asked, shaking hands, " that the connection's gone? "

" Quite! "

Mrs. Pontypool sat down. " It needs heroism in the country," she explained, " to keep sight of anybody."

" Certainly. Crusading, and without a car——"

" Crusading, dear Mrs. Barrow! Yet how did one's ancestors get along? "

" I don't know," Mrs. Barrow said. " It's so rare, isn't it? nowadays, to find anybody who had a grandmother."

" In the times I mean," Mrs. Pontypool said, undismayed, " women went for miles in a sedan-chair, and crossed continents in their tilburies, and in their britschkas, and in their cabriolets! "

" Heroic! "

" Less heroic, surely, than those women one sometimes sees who fasten their bath-chairs to their lovers' auto-bicycles."

" And where have you been—if it isn't indiscreet . . .? "

" We've been spending a few hours at Castle Barbarous."

" I hear Lord Brassknocker is going to open his pictures to the public," Mrs. Shamefoot said. " He has, of course, a very fine Ruisdael, an attractive Sisley and a charming Crome, but really the rest of the collection is only fit for the Sacristy scene in *Manon*."

" A Last Supper at *two tables*," Mrs. Pontypool said confidentially, " struck one as—scarcely——"

" Not if it was Veronese."

" It was Rubens."

" The busiest man who ever lived most certainly was Rubens."

" Was it a party? " Mrs. Barrow asked, less from

63

curiosity than because she would be glad to have something to say to Sartorious during dinner.

Oh, the trial of those dreary dinners at Dawn. . . . What wonder was it that Mrs. Barrow should sometimes become peevish or invent things that were untrue or, in her extremity, hear the Raven's croak? Had she been neurasthenic she would have probably sometimes screamed at the sight of her Lord enjoying an artichoke, slowly, leaf by leaf.

" Was it a party? " Mrs. Barrow asked again.

" Only old Mr. James and little Mrs. Kilmurry," Mrs. Pontypool replied. " Such a strange old man, who strolled once with the Tennysons in the Cascine in Florence."

There was a pause—just long enough for an angel to pass, flying slowly.

" Was Lord Susan there? " Mrs. Barrow inquired.

" He very seldom is," Miss Pontypool said.

" Unfortunate young man," Mrs. Pontypool exclaimed, playing with the tails of her stole; " perpetually he's on the verge of . . . and, although I'm told he's gun-shy, in my opinion . . . and I would willingly have sent a wreath, . . . only where's the use in sending one the day afterwards? "

" But you've heard nothing? "

" No. . . . Naturally the Brassknockers don't care to talk of it before they're quite obliged; but Lady Brassknocker did strike me as being so unusually distrait. Didn't you think so, Queenie? "

" I really didn't notice," Miss Pontypool said. " Where's Goosey? "

" To be sure! I thought if Lord Brassknocker could only see the boy he might take a fancy to him," Mrs. Pontypool said.

" Really, in what way? " Mrs. Barrow wondered.

" Who can tell? Lord Brassknocker's a very important man."

64

" He is a very rich one."

" Poor child! What is one to do with him? In any other age, of course, he could have ambled along in the retinue of some great lady."

" Oh, be thankful," Mrs. Barrow began.

" As it is, with a little influence, he's hoping to get into some garage."

" Poor young man," Mrs. Shamefoot said, with sympathy, " such a bending life! "

By the time the train reached Totterdown Mrs. Barrow congratulated herself that she would be artichoke-proof now, positively, for nearly a week.

In the railway carriage, Mrs. Shamefoot was sufficiently fortunate, too, to secure the seat opposite to herself for a magnificent image of the god Ptah.

The terrific immobility of Egyptian things enchanted her, particularly in the train.

Often the god had aroused her friendliest feelings by saving her from the strain of answering questions, or expressing hopes, or guessing whether the carriage would be there to meet them, or whether it would not, or from the alternative miseries of migraine brought on by feigning to read, for, as Mrs. Shamefoot was aware, she might be called upon to remove a dressing-case, but how seldom did it occur to anyone to deplace a god.

But Mrs. Pontypool was not to be suppressed.

" I once met a Mrs. Asp," she said, " who was writing the life of Hepshepset, wife and sister of Thothmes II, who, on becoming a widow, invented a hairwash and dressed as a man."

The beautiful summer's day had crumbled to dusk as the twin towers of the Cathedral and the short spire (which was, perhaps, an infelicity) came into view.

How desolate it appeared across the fields of wan white clover, now that the sun had gone! Saint Apollinaris in Classe never looked more alone.

" Ashringford is quite a healthy place, isn't it? "
Mrs. Shamefoot inquired anxiously, turning towards
Mrs. Barrow.

Mrs. Barrow opened her eyes.

" One wouldn't care to say so," she replied, " there's
usually a good deal of sickness about; *of a kind.*"

" I consider it a regular doctors' town! " Mrs.
Pontypool exclaimed; " the funeral horses are always
on the go."

Mrs. Pontypool looked humane.

" Poor animals! " she said.

" You see the Ashringford houses are so old,"
Goosey explained, " and so stuffy, and the windows
are so small. It's as if the Ashringford people had made
them themselves by poking a finger through the brick."

" Which makes us all delicate, of course, and the
climate doubly treacherous," Mrs. Pontypool said.
" Although at one time I fancy it used not to be so
bad. I date the change to Bishop Henedge. He was so
High Church. His views were so extremely high!
Quite unintentionally, perhaps, he attracted towards
us the uncertain climate of Rome. I should advise
anyone visiting Ashringford for the first time to do
precisely as they would there."

" And what is that? " Mrs. Shamefoot demanded
doubtfully.

" Wear an extra flannel petticoat."

Much to Mrs. Barrow's disappointment, there was
no Sartorious to meet the train; only a footman—
Lady Georgia's chauffeur attended to Mrs. Shamefoot
and her maid.

" I wonder she keeps him," Mrs. Barrow observed,
as she climbed into her brougham. " From the marks
on his cheeks he looks as if he had been in more than
one break up."

" My regards to Lady Georgia," Goosey called
after Mrs. Shamefoot to say.

" My dear, at nineteen has one regards? " Mrs.
Pontypool said. " Silly, affected boy! "

Mrs. Shamefoot was glad to be alone. How wonderful it was to breathe the evening air. As she sped
towards Stockingham over a darkening plain, patched
with clumps of heavy hyacinthine trees, almost she
could catch the peculiar aroma of the Cathedral.

" As indefinable as piety! " she exclaimed, drawing
on her glove.

VII

LADY ANNE PANTRY was sitting in the china-cupboard, a room fitted with long glass shelves, on which her fabled Dresden figures, monkey musicians, and sphinx marquises, made perfect blots of colour against the gold woodwork of the walls.

Heedless of her sister-in-law, she was reading her morning letters whilst massaging her nose.

" Such a dull post, Anne," that person exclaimed, lifting up an incomparable, tearful, spiritual and intellectual face from the perusal of a circular.

" Mine is not," said Lady Anne.

" Indeed? "

Lady Anne rustled her skirt.

" . . . Mrs. Henedge," she said, " it appears, has quite gone over to Rome."

" But is it settled? "

" Since she's to build in our midst a bijou church for Monsignor Parr. . . . Such scenes, I expect, there'll be."

" Certainly. If it's to be another Gothic fake."

" And Lady Georgia asks if she may lunch here to-morrow and bring a Mrs. Shamefoot. Mysteries with the Bishop. And there's been *almost* a murder at the workhouse again."

" How very disgraceful."

" And the Twyfords are coming—at least some of them. Less tiresome, perhaps, than if they all came at once."

" I love her postscripts——"

" To-day there isn't one. And that brocade, you remember, I liked, is seventy shillings a yard."

" Too dear."

" And I said *a spot*, Aurelia; I did not say a *cart-wheel* . . ." Lady Anne murmured, getting up to display her wares.

Lady Anne had turned all her troubles to beauty, and at forty-five she had an interesting face. She was short and robust, with calm, strong features, and in the evening she sometimes suggested Phèdre. Her voice was charming, full of warmth and colour, and although she did not sing, it might be said of her that she was a mute soprano.

Aurelia Pantry extended a forlorn and ravishing hand.

" Aren't they fools? " she exclaimed, spreading out the materials before her.

She spoke habitually rather absently, as though she were placing the last brick to some gorgeous castle in the air.

It was the custom at the Palace that the Bishop's eleven sisters should spend a month in rotation there each year.

Aurelia, who was the most popular (being the least majestical, the least like Eleanor), corresponded, as a rule, to August and September.

Of the Bishop's eleven sisters, indeed, she was the only one that Lady Anne could endure.

Eleanor, Ambrosia, Hypolita, Virginia, Prudence, Lettice, Chrissy, Patsy, Gussy and Grace were all shocking, hopeless and dreadful, according to Lady Anne.

But Aurelia, who was just a little mystic, added a finish, a distinction to the Palace; especially got up in muslin, when, like some sinuous spirit, she could appear so ethereal as to be almost a flame.

" I think, of course, it's perfect," Miss Pantry said, holding her head aslant *like smoke in the wind*, as she considered the stuff, " but the design limits it."

69

" I should call it hardly modest myself."

" There's something always so inconsecutive, isn't there, about a spot? "

" But a spot, Aurelia; in theory, what *could* be quieter? "

" Nothing, dear," Miss Pantry said.

" And yet," Lady Anne murmured, " when one's fastening one's mind on one's prayers, one requires a little something."

" I cannot see why it should be easier to sink into a brown study by staring at a splash."

" Often, I think it helps."

" Of course you may be right."

" Shall we take it down into the Cathedral, Anne, and try? "

" This morning I've so many things to do. There's always one's small share of mischief going on."

" I would never take part in the parish broils if ever I could avoid it."

" I cannot be so impersonal, I'm afraid."

" But surely a little neutral sympathy——"

" To be sympathetic without discrimination is so very debilitating."

" Do you never feel tired? "

" Oh yes, sometimes."

" I adore the country," Aurelia said, " but I should die of weariness if I stayed here long."

" No, really, I like Ashringford. I abuse it, of course, just as I do dear Walter, or anybody whom I see every day . . . but really I'm fond of the place."

" That's quite reasonable."

" And if sometimes I'm a wreck," Lady Anne explained, " I look forward to my St. Martin's summer later on."

" But Canterbury's so dreadful. It's such a groove."

" The proximity of our English Channel would be a joy."

" It's only seldom you'd get a whiff of the sea."
Lady Anne's eyes skimmed her lawn.

A conventional bird or two—a dull thrush, a glossy crow—cowering for worms; what else had she, or anyone else, the right to expect? Sun, wind and quivering leaves made a carpet of moving shadows.

" It's with Stockingham," she said, " at present, that I've a bone. I shall scold Lady Georgia when she comes. To tell a curate his profile is suggestive of Savonarola is so like her. But it's really a mistake. It makes a man firebrand, even when he's not. He gets rude and makes pointed remarks, and offends everybody. And I have to sit at home to talk to him."

Aurelia looked interested.

" Probably a creature with a whole gruesome family? " she indirectly inquired.

" Unhappily he's only just left Oxford."

" Ah, handsome, then, I hope."

" On the contrary, he's like one of those cherubs one sees on eighteenth-century fonts with their mouths stuffed with cake."

" Not really? "

"*And he wears glasses.*"

" But he takes them off sometimes——? "

" That's just what I don't know."

" Then, as you will hardly need me," Aurelia said, " I'll go over to the Cresswell Arms and see Chloe. Poor dear, it's very dull for her all alone."

" How is Miss Valley getting on? "

" So well. She asks if she can come up one afternoon to examine the tapestries when Walter's out."

" By all means, but the tapestries are too fantastic, I should imagine, to be of any service to her. Historically, they're quite . . . untrustworthy."

" Does it matter? Besides, the Archdeacon believes that Mrs. Cresswell was an Ely anchoress and not an Ashringford anchoress at all."

" That's nonsense," Lady Anne said; " she belongs to us."

" I don't know why you should be so keen on her," Miss Pantry said. " Of course, she *may* have been a saint, but from some of the little things I've heard, I fancy you might ransack heaven to find her——"

" I won't hear anything against Mrs. Cresswell. Her career here was an exquisite example to us all."

" Well, I'm sure I hope so, dear."

" And perhaps, Aurelia," Lady Anne said gently, " if you're going to the Cresswell Arms you'll call at the workhouse on your way, and find out what actually took place. I won't ask you to stop in Priest Street with a pudding. . . . And if you should see Miss Hospice in the garden, will you send her up to me? "

For some time after Aurelia had left her, Lady Anne stood in the window looking out upon the Cathedral. There was usually a little scaffolding about it. . . . If she had a voice in the matter it should never be allowed to come away. Her spirit shrank from the peculiar oppressiveness of perfection. And the Cathedral was very perfect indeed. How admirable, through the just sufficient drapery of the trees, were the great glazed windows that flashed like black diamonds in the sun. The glass, indeed, at Ashringford was so wonderful that sticks and umbrellas were left (by order) at the door. . . .

Lady Anne looked up at the large contented towers and fetched a sigh.

They were lovely.

Without veiling her eyes, they were as near perfection as she could conveniently bear. Placed at the end of the tennis lawn too, they had saved her from many a run.

Miss Missingham, in her *Sacerdotalism and Satanism,* has called the whole thing heavy, "*Very weighty indeed,*" although she willingly admits that at twilight the towers, with their many pinnacles, become utterly fantastic, *like the helmets of eunuchs in carnival time*. But then, if there was not much spontaneity about them on the whole, they had taken so long to build. Stone towers cannot be dashed off like Fragonard's *Inspiration*.

At the Pilgrims' Depot in the busy High Street there is to be obtained an anthology of " Last Words," culled chiefly from the lips of the womenkind of the Episcopal set. If the sayings of these ladies were often salty and frequently pointed, the Palace, it should be said, faced a Gothic arch.

Built around two sides of a quadrangle, it was, according to local taste, an ugly, forlorn affair, its bricks having been masked by stucco in 1785. Here and there, where the stucco had chipped away, the brick peeped out as if some rare fresco lay smothered underneath. From a flagged courtyard a classic staircase of divine proportions swept, exteriorly, to a broad balcony above the ground floor (spoken of sometimes as the loggia), which created, perhaps, something of a grand-opera effect.

It was here, recumbent upon a deck-chair, propped up by piles of brilliant cushions, that Mrs. Henedge, in her day, preferred to drink afternoon tea, surrounded by the most notable Church dignitaries that she could find.

It was told that at one of these courts she had had as many as three bishops simultaneously handing her toast.

What wonder was it that persons should linger in delighted amazement at the wrought-iron gates until they formed a substantial crowd?

Carts would draw up, motorists stop, pedestrians sit down.

Lady Anne, on the contrary, preferred to hold her receptions out of sight.

To many, unquestionably it was a blow.

73

She preferred, when not indoors, her tennis lawn, with its high clipped hedges, behind which the Cathedral rose inscrutably, a soft grey pile elongating itself above the trees, from whence would fall, fitfully, the saintly caw-cawing of the rooks.

Lady Anne's eyes fell from the wise old towers.

Framed in the expiring windows of the china-cupboard, the glimpse of Ashringford was entrancing quite. Across the meadows could be seen the struggling silver of the broad river, as it curled about Crawbery, invariably with some enthusiast, rod in hand, waiting quietly upon the bank. Nearer, hither and thither, appeared a few sleepy spires of churches, too sensible to compete with the Cathedral, but nevertheless possibly more personal; like the minor characters in repertoire that support the star.

She turned as her secretary, Miss Hospice, entered.

With a rather cruel yellow at her neck, waist and feet, and a poem of fifty sheets, on *Verlaine at Bournemouth*, at her back. What is there left to say——

Lady Anne was fond of her secretary because of her wild, beautiful handwriting, that seemed to fly, and because she really did enjoy to snub the Bishop's sisters. And others, too, liked her. Perpetually, she would make those pleasant little pampered remarks, such as, on a sultry August night, " B-r-r-r! it's cold enough to light a fire! " Now that Aurelia was at the Palace, she should have been away on holiday, but, somehow, this year, she wasn't.

Lady Anne had discovered Miss Hospice some years since, lost in the advertisements of *The Spectator* seeking, as she had explained, the position of guardian angel to some elderly literary man.

Intelligent and sympathetic, Nature had appeared to indicate the way. The short hair, the long wavy nose *à la* Luca Signorelli, that seemed scarcely willing to sustain the heavy gold glasses, the figure, as flat as

74

Lower Egypt, and the dazzling eyes like Mrs. Aphra Behn—for a really ticklish post, all was right. With complete clairvoyance Lady Anne had secured this treasure for her own, whose secretarial uses had now quite reached their zenith. Miss Madge Hospice was Lady Anne's barbed wire.

" I was wondering what had become of you," Lady Anne said to her as she came in. " Where on earth have you been? "

" . . . Wading through fields of violet vetch. It's so delicious out."

" Had you forgotten to-day? "

" I don't think so: I've told Gripper again to sponge the stretchers, but he's so lazy, you know he never will."

The bi-weekly Ambulance Classes at the Palace, so popular socially, were, it must be owned, on a parallel with the butter-making at Trianon.

" That's thoughtful," Lady Anne said. " And now, here are so many letters to answer, I really don't know where to begin."

When a few minutes later the Reverend Peter Pet was announced they were entirely engrossed.

"Savonarola! " Lady Anne exclaimed. Miss Hospice continued conscientiously to write.

" Is it possible that anybody cares a straw what he says? " she queried.

" A curate should be quiescent; that's the first thing."

" But tactlessness is such a common complaint."

" He has referred to the Bishop as *a Faun crowned with roses*," Lady Anne said severely.

" I *heard* it was *Satyr*."

" And his encounter with Miss Wookie. . . . Well, not since the last election have I heard anything so scurrilous."

" And is he absolutely charming? "

75

Lady Anne arranged her descriptions; when the introductions came about there was often some confusion.

"He's fair," she said, "with bright green eyes. And such gay, attractive teeth."

"You make me curious to see him."

"I should hate to shake his faith in his vocation," Lady Anne murmured, "but——"

"Have you dropped anything?"

"Only my little bit of lace. . . ."

And although very likely Lady Anne was the most sensible woman alive, she would scarcely have had the claim had she not crossed first to the mirror and——

But oh, *Vanity!* is there any necessity to explain?

VIII

"How fond I am of this sleepy magic place!"

"In town," Mrs. Shamefoot said, "the trees so seldom forget themselves into expressive shapes."

"Well . . . You haven't answered my question yet."

"Because I don't know!"

Lord Blueharnis looked bored.

"Is it grey," Lady Castleyard wondered, chiming in, "or white; or would it be blue?"

She settled herself reposefully, as if for ever.

"That Sacharissa style," Atalanta remarked, bending forward, "of rolling your hair is so enslaving."

"I wish you would *not* look down my neck like an archer of Carpaccio."

"Tell me what you're guessing."

"The colour of the cuckoo's egg. . . ."

"If I recollect, it's a mystic medley of mauves."

Mrs. Shamefoot prepared to rise. "We shall get appendicitis," she exclaimed, "if we sit here long."

Lord Blueharnis prevented her. "Oh, what charming hands! . . . Don't move."

"If you admire them now," Mrs. Shamefoot said, sinking back, "you would worship them when I'm really worn out. My hands never look quite so marvellous as when I'm tired."

"But . . . fresh as you are; mayn't I see?"

"How perfectly idiotic you are."

"For years," Lady Georgia's voice came falling to them through the dusk, "she couldn't get rid of it. In the end, quite in despair, and simply prostrate, she exchanged it for a string of pearls."

"Might one learn what?" Lord Blueharnis inquired, half turning.

"Number 39. . . . Her great, comfortless house."

"Darling Georgia! Why will she always withdraw to the gladiators' seats?"

"Away, too, in all the dew."

"'Up in those tracts with her, it was the peace of utter light and silence.'"

"How fascinating your *cabochon* tips look, dear, against the night."

"Little horrid—owl—thing, I wonder you can see them at all."

"How astonishingly acoustic it is."

"These marble tiers are very cold."

"I don't suppose the Greeks wore any more than we do."

"Though, possibly, not less."

"Aren't you coming down to recite?"

"Oh no; when Miss Compostella comes, we'll get her to do it instead."

"I shall come up and fetch you," Mrs. Shamefoot said, "if Mr. Aston will lend me a hand."

And, with the indifference of Madame Valpy about to climb the scaffold, she rose.

She was wearing an imaginative plain white dress that made her appear like a broken statue.

"Good-bye," she murmured, "Dirce," her voice harking to the period of her heels—Louis XV.

"Be very careful. I've had Aase's Death Music running in my head all day. . . ."

And now beneath her lay the Greek theatre like an open fan. All around the glimmering sweeps of steps the sullen elms gave a piquant English touch.

"How perfectly fairy!" she exclaimed, falling breathless at the top.

Like some thin archangel, Lady Georgia stooped to help her rise.

"I adore the end of summer," she said, "when a new haystack appears on every hill."

Beyond the dark proscenium and the clustering chimneys of the house stretched the faint far fields. No lofty peaks, or Himalayas, but quiet, modest hills, a model of restraint.

"Isn't it soothing?" Mrs. Shamefoot said.

"I suppose so; but it quite makes me cry to think of you fastened up over there in Ashringford, with a stiff neck, till the day of doom."

"I always respond," Mrs. Shamefoot replied, "to the sun."

Lady Georgia opened wide, liquid eyes. "I shall hardly ever dare to come and look at you," she said.

"But I should be entirely flattering, dear, for you."

"Would you? Many people are so thoughtless about their lights."

Mrs. Shamefoot wound an arm about the neck of an architectural figure.

"Don't you agree," she said, "that there's something quite irresistible about stained-glass caught in a brutality of stone?"

Lady Georgia seated herself stiffly. "Caught," she exclaimed. "When I die, I should prefer to leave no trace."

"But you follow, darling, don't you, what I mean?"

"For anyone that needed a perpetual retreat," Lady Georgia said, "Ashringford, I should say, would be quite ideal. The choir's so good. Such peaceful voices. . . . And there's nothing about the Cathedral in any way forbidding! One could really hardly wish for anything *nicer*. The late Bishop often used to say it suggested to him *Siena*, with none of the sickening scent of hides."

Mrs. Shamefoot became ecstatic.

"We must make Dr. Pantry promise a two-tier window," she said, "and Dirce can take the top."

"Sharing a window," Lady Georgia said, "in my opinion, is such a mistake. One might just as well erect a Jesse-window and invite a whole multitude to join. It may be egotistical, but if I were going down the centuries at all, I should want to go alone."

"Unfortunately," Mrs. Shamefoot murmured, "it's too late to alter things, without behaving badly. ..."

"That could be arranged. There's not the same rush now for monuments that there used to be."

"Just at present there's almost a revival. . . . There are so many Art Schools about, aren't there? Everybody one meets appears to be commemorating themselves in one way or another. It's become a craze. Only the other day my mother-in-law had designed for Soco a tiny triptych of herself as a kind of Madonna, with a napkin drawn far down over her eyes."

"Really?"

"Of course it's only a firescreen; it's *certain* to get scorched."

"But still——"

"And with some scraps of old Flemish glass Lady Faningay has set up a sort of tortoise-shell window to a friend; so pretty. . . . She would have it."

"Oh, that dreadful réchauffé of fragments. I've seen it."

"But you understand, don't you, dearest, my poor motives, what they mean. . . ."

"I should be disappointed," Lady Georgia said, "if you did not, with Mrs. Cresswell, become the glory of the town." And with a sorrowful, sidelong smile she turned towards Ashringford, admirable in a gay glitter of lights.

Faint as rubbed-out charcoal where it touched the sky, loomed the Cathedral, very wise and very old, and very vigilant and very detached—like a diplomat in disgrace—its towers, against the orange dusk, swelling saliently towards their base, inflated, so the guide-books said, by the sweet music of Palestrina. Between them, an exquisite specimen of irony, careered the short spire, which was perhaps an infelicity that would grow all long and regretful-looking towards the night.

" Since you've climbed so far," Lady Georgia said, " I shall repeat to you a somewhat saturnine little song of Mrs. Cresswell."

And opening her fan, she said:

" I am disgusted with Love.
 I find it exceedingly disappointing,
 Mine is a nature that cries for more ethereal things,
 Banal passions fail to stir me.
 I am disgusted with Love."

" How heavenly she is! "
" Such an amusing rhythm——"
" I do so enjoy the bypaths," Mrs. Shamefoot said, " of poetry. Isn't there any more? "
" No. I believe that's all."
" Of course her words condemn her."
" But that she should have arrived at a state of repugnance, possibly, is something."
" Isn't it unkind," Lady Castleyard interrupted, advancing towards them, " to recite up here all alone?"
" Dearest Dirce, how silently you came!——"
" Like a cook we had on the Nile," Lady Georgia observed, " who once startled me more than I can ever say by breaking suddenly out of the moon-mist so noiselessly that he might have been treading on a cloud."
" Well, won't you come down? A stage and nobody on it is shockingly dull."
" This evening, I really don't feel equal to Euripides," Lady Georgia murmured, " although perhaps I might manage the *Hound*."

" *The Hound of Heaven?* My dear, what could be more divine? "

Mrs. Shamefoot looked away.

Star beyond star, the sky was covered. The clouds, she observed, too, appeared to be preparing for an Assumption.

I X

WHEN Aurelia left Lady Anne she set a straw hat harmlessly upon her head, powdered her neck at a tarnished mirror with crystal nails, selected a violet parasol, profoundly flounced, slipped a small volume of Yogi Philosophy into her wallet, took up, put down, and finally took up the cornflour pudding, gave a tearful final glance at her reflection, put out her tongue for no remarkable reason, and walked out into the street.

Oh, these little expeditions through the town! . . .

Hypolita habitually got over them by horse when, in a bewildering amazon, she would swoop away like a valkyrie late for a sabbat.

"One can only hope that heaven will wash," Aurelia murmured meekly, as she prepared to trudge. Which optimism, notwithstanding the perfect stillness of the day, fluttered her aside like a leaf.

It was disgraceful the way her linen came home —torn.

"Torn, torn, torn," she breathed, twirling her sunshade with short, sharp twirls that implied the click of a revolver.

But to reach the laundry she was obliged to pass the Asz—that river spoken of, by vulgar persons, often, as *the Ass*.

Between solemn stone embankments and an array of bridges spaced out with effigies of fluminal deities, a sadly spent river coiled reluctant through the town. Sensitive townsfolk felt intensely this absence of water, which, in many minds, amounted almost to a disgrace. Before the Cathedral, just where, artistically, it was needed most, there was scarcely a trickle.

As a rule Aurelia was too completely preoccupied with her own sensations to observe particularly her whereabouts, but instinctively, as her foot touched the bridge, she would assume the tiresome, supercilious smile of a visitor.

This morning, however, she paused to lean an arm upon the parapet to rest her pudding.

Has not Mrs. Cresswell (in a trance) described heaven as *another* grim reality? Aurelia stood, and remained to drum a tune.

" Oh, I could dance for ever," she exclaimed, " to the valse from *Love Fifteen!* " And she lingered to hum, by way of something more, Priscilla's air from *Th' Erechtheum Miss.* How giddy it was! What abandon there was in it. Happy Priscilla, hardworking little thing; from her part song with Bill, love, manifestly, was sometimes simple and satisfactory.

Aurelia peered down.

The creak of oarswhispered up to her with wizardry.

There was often a barge to be towed along. Here came one now, lifted over the sun-splashed water, with a mast, long and slightly bent, like the quill of an ostrich feather. The stubby willows, that mirrored their cloudy shadows from the bank, sobbed pathetically, though too well bred to weep.

" It gets emptier and emptier," she mused. " I suppose the weeds absorb the water! "

" Oh, beware of freckles! "

Aurelia turned.

" Who could have foreseen," she said, " that our intercession for fine weather would produce all this heat? "

" If two of the churches, in future, were to apply, I consider it should amply suffice." And Mrs. Henedge, leaning leisurely upon the arm of Winsome Brookes, and sharing the weight of half a mysterious basket with Monsignor Parr, nodded and was gone.

With her streaming strings and veils she suggested, from behind, the Goddess Hathor as a sacred cow. "I'd rather go naked than wear some of the things she wears," Aurelia murmured critically, as she watched her out of sight. But a ripple of laughter from some persons at the toll made Miss Pantry fix her eyes perseveringly into space. The peals of laughter of the Miss Chalfonts were as much a part of Ashringford as the Cathedral bells. Constantly they were laughing. And nobody knew why. Along the crooked High Street they were often to be seen, almost speechless with merriment, peering in at the shop windows, a trio interlaced, or standing before the announcements of the Lilliputian Opera House, where came never anything more extraordinarily exhilarating than Moody-Manners or Mrs. D'Oyley Carte. Tourists avoided their collision. And even the delicate-looking policeman in the market-place, when he became aware of their approach, would invariably disappear.

Rossetti, long ago, had painted them, very pale, in bunched-up dresses, playing cats'-cradle in a grey primeval waste. And the reaction, it was politely supposed, had completely turned their brain.

"They will laugh themselves to death," Aurelia murmured, as she wandered on.

The scent of the bushes of sweetbrier from innumerable gardens followed her along the sentimental esplanade that faced the Asz as far as the gates of Miss Chimney's school for backward boys. Here Vane Street, with its model workhouse, began, the admiration of all. Debt, disaster, held few terrors, while gazing at this winter palace. . . . With a chequered pavement below, and an awning above, a man, trusting to philanthropy, might reasonably aspire to lounge away what remained to him of life, inhaling the suavest of cigarettes.

Deferring her errand there until her return, Aurelia wound up Looking-Glass Street towards the laundry. With its houses, that seemed to have been squeezed from tubes of multi-coloured paint, it was not unlike, she had often heard, a street in one of Goldoni's plays. Miss Hospice catches the peeping Brueghelness of it in her *Scroll from the Fingers of Ta-Hor*, in which, steeping herself in deception and mystery, she attempts to out-Chatterton Chatterton with:

" Poor pale pierrot through the dark boughs peering
　In the purple gloaming of a summer's evening,
　Oh his heart is breaking, can't you hear him sobbing,
　Or is it the wind that's passing among the yellow
　　roses? . . ."

An imperfect scarab that owed its existence chiefly from loitering in Looking-Glass Street, or thereabouts.

Choosing her way along it, Aurelia perceived, midway, a lady with a pair of scissors, who, in an abstracted attitude, was inducing a yew-tree peacock to behave.

" Good-morning," the lady with the scissors cried, " I am so glad. . . . I was just coming round to inquire."

Miss Wookie was always *just going* somewhere. At all hours one would find her in a hat.

" To inquire? " Aurelia halted.

The lady leaned classically against her bird. In its rather dishevelled state, it resembled a degenerate swan.

" People are circulating such dreadful stories," she said.

" Indeed! "

" Such shocking stories. Poor mamma! This morning she seems quite pulled down."

" Some new nervousness, no doubt."

" She has sent me out to tidy this. As if I were in a condition for gardening! "

" To fulfil a ritual, if one isn't quite oneself, does often only harm."

Miss Wookie considered her work. " I clip the thing," she said, " in the wrong places. . . . In profile it has almost the look of a turkey. So unnatural! "

" Whatever happens, it could always be a blue bird."

" We hear you're going to pull down half of the Cathedral," Miss Wookie said tragically, " and put in a Russian ballet window. Is it *true?* "

Aurelia appeared astonished.

" It's the first I've heard of it! " she exclaimed.

" The Palace, of course, always is the last to hear of anything," Miss Wookie said, " but I assure you all Ashringford's talking. And, *oh, Miss Pantry,* Mr. Pet has been saying the most frightful things about us. About me, and about mamma."

" He's a horrid, conceited boy," Aurelia comforted her.

" Come in, won't you? I'd like you to hear the truth."

Aurelia blinked. " It's very kind," she said, " but with this nasty, sticky dish——"

" Never mind the dish," Miss Wookie murmured, unlatching the gate.

" Sycamores," the shelter of Mrs. Wookie, the widow of Brigadier Percy Wookie of the Ashringford Volunteers, to whom there was an explanatory tablet in St. Cyriac's which related, like a page torn from Achilles Tatius, how and where, and by whose manicured extremities he fell, was a bleak brick cottage, with " 1839 " scrawled above the door. A short path with a twist like a lizard's tail led up to the entrance, where an unremarkable tree with a long Latin name did its best to keep out the light.

87

" Poor, poor, poor, *poor* mamma! " Miss Wookie repeated rhythmically, as she led the way in.

Mrs. Wookie was usually to be found reclining upon a sofa, agitating a phial of medicine, or embroidering martyrdoms imaginatively upon a stole. Interrupted in any way, she would become as flurried as a canary when a hand is thrust into its cage.

But to-day, because she was unwell, her daughter had given her, by way of distraction, a party frock to pull to pieces, and now the invalid was aggrandising perceptibly the aperture to an evening gown in a posture rather more at ease than that of Whistler's Mother.

The morning-room at the " Sycamores," mid-Victorian and in the Saracen style, would most likely have impressed a visitor as an act of faith throughout. Upon the mantelshelf, however, between much that was purely emigrant, stood two strange bottles.

Being in the City-of-Random-Kisses to receive a legacy, and by proxy (alas) a blessing; and caught in a shower of perhaps pre-determined rain, Miss Wookie and her guardian angels—handsome rural creatures— had sought shelter beneath the nearest arch.

It was noon. All three were completely wet.

" Christie's . . ." Miss Wookie observed the name, whilst the angels shook the water from their hair, and flapped the moisture sparkling from their wings. And reassured by the six first letters, she had gone inside.

" What else? " she can recall remarking, prepared for a waiter to pounce out upon her from the top of the stairs.

And then, instead of the prosaic bone, as afterwards she explained, and the glass of lemonade, and the quiet rest, and the meditation on the unexpected behaviour of poor Aunt Nettle . . . Miss Wookie had found herself calling out in a sort of dream for the vases, until, for the life of her, it would have been impossible to stop. And when, ultimately, she reappeared in Ashringford, the legacy all gone, it never occurred to Mrs. Wookie to part with her *famille rose* again.

"Family Rose" the bottles had become to her—and accordingly as dear.

"I see that bodices are getting more and more scamped, Kate," Mrs. Wookie remarked, as her daughter came in, "and so, my dear, I hope I've done what's right."

Miss Wookie ſtood ſtill. "Oh, Tatty," she said.

"With the scraps of ſtuff I've taken," Mrs. Wookie announced, "I can make four small pincushions; or two large ones."

"I didn't know how selfish you could be."

"Don't be absurd, Kate. You may be sure I'd not allow you to appear in anything unbecoming. And if you go out, my child, to-night, don't forget, like laſt time, to order yourself *a fly*."

"I'm so glad," Aurelia murmured, coming forward, "you're able to sew."

With her needle suspended in the air, Mrs. Wookie fluttered off to a favourite perch.

"I was very poorly firſt thing," she said. "Kate tried to persuade me to send for a physician. But I wouldn't let her."

"Luckily an attack is quickly gone."

Mrs. Wookie began to twitter. "And one of these days," she observed, "I'll go with it. I hardly expeɑt to survive the fall of the leaf; I don't see how I can. . . . Shall you ever forget laſt year, Kate? Round Ashringford, there're so many trees."

"Possibly all you need's a change of scene. Scheveningen, or somewhere——"

Mrs. Wookie floated to the floor. "A few minutes more or less on earth," she said dejeɑtedly, "what does it matter? And packing upsets me so. Besides, I wish to die here, beneath my own roof."

" But what pleasure would it give you? "

" None, Miss Pantry. But I wish to die there."

" You may be right," Aurelia assented; " the strained atmosphere of tuberose and trunks of a health resort in autumn is often a little sad."

" And Ashringford in autumn," Miss Wookie said, "isn't so bad. Of course the leaves come down. The worst of it is, one can get no grapes; I can get no grapes."

Mrs. Wookie looked pathetic. " If I could only see Kate married," she complained. " It comes, of course, of living in a cathedral town. Curates are such triflers."

" One little wedding, Mrs. Wookie, oughtn't to be so difficult. Consider, with five or six daughters to dispose of, how much more tiresome it would have been! "

At such a notion Mrs. Wookie's nose grew almost long.

" In the forties," she crooned, " we were always dropping our things, and we fainted more. Of course, in the country there are many ways still. One can send a girl out with a landscape figure, sketching. That always works. . . . Alice, Grace, Pamela and Teresa, my nieces, all went that way."

" Oh, Tatty, Teresa married a menial. She went away with a chauffeur."

" How very disgraceful! " Aurelia remarked.

" I suppose it was. Particularly as he wasn't their own."

" Be quiet, my dear; we live too near the laundry as it is."

" Besides," Miss Wookie said, striking her chord, " I don't intend to marry. I should be sorry to let myself in for so many miseries. . . . An habitual husband would, also, bore me to death."

" Hush, Kate! It's just those infantine reflections that circulate and get twisted, till they arrive, goodness knows how, to the ears of that dreadful Mr. Pet."

"I'm sorry you find him so troublesome," Aurelia said.

Mrs. Wookie glowered. "I wonder I'm alive," she exclaimed, "from the reports they bring. Not only am I affronted, but the Cathedral, it seems, itself, is in peril, and the name of our city also endangered. For a whim, if not from sheer madness, Dr. Pantry, it appears, has petitioned the Archbishop to contract the See of Ashringford into *Ashingford*. Merciful heaven, why can't he leave it alone?"

"I dare say if Mr. Pet had his way he would boil us down to *Ash*," Miss Wookie observed.

Her mother closed her eyes.

"If that happened," she said, "I should leave Ashringford."

Driven out with her Family Rose, and followed by her servant Quirker, and by Kate, she saw herself stumbling at sunset like the persecuted women on her stoles. And night would find them (who knew) where the cornflowers passed through the fields in a firm blue bar.

"That Mr. Pet is a disgrace to his cloth," she murmured, rallying. "Indeed, I'd rather we had Mr. Cunningham back again. He wasn't a great preacher, but he neither droned nor gabbled, and he could be wonderfully voluble when he liked."

"Oh, my dear, but he was so unbalanced. He would do his American conjuring tricks in the vestry before the choir boys. . . . Such a bad example."

"Still, it's an ill wind. . . . And Miss Wardle and her set seem quite satisfied with his successor."

"She would be. If you asked her for her hymn-book she'd imagine it was being borrowed for some felonious purpose."

Aurelia looked interested. "I don't see what one could do with a hymn-book," she exclaimed.

Mrs. Wookie's nose grew long again.

" Don't you? " she answered. " Neither do I."

" Besides, fresh from a Cornish curacy, what can he know? " Miss Wookie wondered.

Aurelia corrected her.

" From Oxford, I fancy, isn't he . . .? "

" The man's a perfect scourge, wherever he's from," Miss Wookie declared. " Not half-an-hour ago he dashed down this street like a tornado. I was standing with Quirker at the door. You know I collect motor numbers, which obliges me frequently to run out into the road. . . . I have such a splendid collection. I hope I'm not so vulgar as to bang a door, still, when I saw him coming, I confess I shut it! "

Mrs. Wookie joined her hands.

" He must have discovered about Mrs. Henedge and Monsignor Parr," she said. " How shocking, should there be a struggle."

" What should make you think so? "

" They've gone to pace out the site of the new church. . . . Monsignor Parr has been hurrying to and fro all the morning, like St. Benedict at Monte Cassino. And his employees already are entrenched at the corner of Whip-me-Whop-me Street at Mrs. Cresswell's old Flagellites Club."

Aurelia raised her eyes.

" Surely in such a sweet old house it would feel almost vulgar to be alive! "

" I don't know," Mrs. Wookie replied. " I do not care for Mrs. Cresswell. She repels me."

"In any case, if anything should happen, Mrs. Henedge will be quite secure. That fair-haired pianist accompanied her. You remember him, don't you, mamma? "

" I remember him perfectly. Nobody in the world ever got over a stile like Mr. Brookes."

" To see her continually with that perverse musician or with that priest is enough to make poor good Bishop Henedge burst his coffin."

" Alas, Ashringford isn't what it used to be," Mrs. Wookie complained. " The late Bishop was, in many matters, perhaps not a very prudent man . . . but he had authority. And a shapelier leg, my dears, never trod the earth. He obtained his preferment, one may say, solely on their account. He had such long, long legs. Such beautiful long, long legs."

" And," Miss Wookie murmured, flinging her flower, " a really reassuring way of blowing his nose! To hear him do it was to realise immediately the exact meaning of *conviction*."

" But in the official portrait," Aurelia objected, " he appears such a little gasp of a man! "

Mrs. Wookie became belligerent.

" That topsy-turvy thing in the Town Hall! I was fond of my husband, but I'd scorn to be painted in evening-mourning pointing at his dead miniature. His portrait indeed! His widow's rather, basking on a sofa, with a locket."

" Apparently Mrs. Henedge admires the baroque."

" Well, her new church will be dedicated to it," Miss Wookie assured.

" So ornate? "

" Mr. Thumbler has gone to Italy to make the drawings. . . . The exterior is to be an absolute replica of St. Thomas in Cremona, with stone saints in demonstrative poses on either side of the door."

" And the interior, no doubt, will be a dream."

" It is to be lit entirely by glass eighteenth-century chandeliers," Miss Wookie said, " and there will be a Pompeian frieze, and a good deal of art leather work from the hand of one of Lady Georgia's young men, who did some of the panelling at St. Anatasia's once, although, of course, he was rather *restricted*."

" Art leather," Aurelia said, " sounds to me a mistake."

93

" If it's half as delicate as at St. Anatasia, it should be really rather lovely."

" Let us hope that it may——"

" And then there are to be some very nice pictures. In fact, the pictures will be a feast. Madame Gandarella, the wife of the Minister, has presented a *St. Cecilia Practising* and a more than usually theatrical Greuze. And Baroness Lützenschläger is to give a Griego. Nobody knows quite what it represents—long, spiritual women grouped about a cot. The Clalfonts, also, are offering a Guardi for the baptistery. But as there was never any mention of one, they ran no very terrible risk. And last, though hardly least, Lord Brassknocker is sending to Paris to be framed a mysterious pastelle entitled *Tired Eyelids on Tired Eyes* which, as Mrs. Pontypool truly says, is certainly the very last thing she looks."

" Kate hears everything," Mrs. Wookie said; " thread me a needle, Kate."

" And when everything is complete, the Grand Duchess Ximina will stay at Stockingham to unveil the leather. The Cardinal Pringle will appear to sprinkle the pictures and to bless it all."

" If the Grand Duchess stays at Stockingham," Mrs. Wookie said, " I suppose they will prepare the State bed."

" Poor woman," Aurelia murmured. " It's as hard as a board."

" Elizabeth——" Miss Wookie began, but Aurelia rose.

" How pretty the garden looks," she said.

Miss Wookie smiled.

" It's only charming," she observed, checked in her little tale, " on account of the trees."

" Tut, Kate. I'm sure in the spring, when the laburnums are out, and lilacs in bloom, the garden's hard to beat."

" It has been always summer," Aurelia said, as she took her leave, " when I've stayed here before."

Down an alley and through an arch led her straight to Washing-tub Square.

Notwithstanding the eloquence prepared, it was with relief that she perceived her laundress docilely pinning some purple flowers against a fence, while close by, in the dust, Miss Valley was kneeling, with her arms about a child.

At her approach the Biographer lifted loose blue eyes that did not seem quite firm in her head, and a literary face.

" I shall have to commence my life all over again," she said. " Six weeks wasted! This child—employed in the laundry here "—and she began to shake it— " this carrier of dirty linen . . . is Reggie . . . Cresswell—a descendant of the saint. . . ."

And because Miss Valley seemed in such distress, and because, after all, she was a friend, Aurelia let fall her dish and, with a glance right and left, first, to make sure that " nothing was coming," sank down upon the road, by her side.

" But can you not see," she murmured sympathetically, taking Miss Valley by the hand, " that an apologia is just what everyone most enjoys? " And then, drawing Reggie to her, she exclaimed: " Oh, you dear little boy! "

X

" AND your own tomb, dear Doctor Pantry, what is it going to be? "

" My own tomb," the Bishop replied demurely, " will be composed entirely of encaustic tiles that come from Portugal—a very simple affair."

Mrs. Shamefoot sighed. " It sounds," she said, " almost agitating."

" Ah, these old cathedrals, my dear Mrs. Shamefoot, how many marriages and funerals they've seen!"

" I suppose——"

" Ashringford may not have the brave appearance of Overcares, or the rhythm of Perch, or the etherealness of Carnage, or the supremacy of Sintrap; but it has a character, a conspicuousness of its own."

" It stands with such authority."

" To be sure. You'd hardly believe there was a debt upon it."

" No; indeed one would not."

Lady Anne broke in. " There is often," she remarked, " a haze. Although I couldn't bear the Cathedral without a few sticks and props, I should miss them frightfully. It's curious the way the restorations hang fire, especially with the number of big houses there are about. Don't you agree with me, Mrs. Roggers? "

" Decidedly," the Archdeacon's wife exclaimed, beginning to docket them upon a glove. When revealing no small mishap, she quite omitted Stockingham from the list.

At this gust of tact Lady Anne appeared amazed.

"If Mrs. Shamefoot wishes to explore the Cathedral,"

the Bishop said, " it will be well to do so before the excursion train gets in from Perch."

" Then you had better take her across."

" But you'll come with us."

" I must remain here for Lady Georgia. Should Mrs. Henedge be out or telling her beads she'll be back directly."

" Very well, we will not be long."

" And be careful," Lady Anne adjured her husband, with fine frankness, " not to commit yourself. No rash promises! The Cathedral's all glass as it is. It will be like a conservatory before we've done."

" What are those wonderfully white roses? " Mrs. Shamefoot inquired of the Bishop, as she trailed with him away.

In a *costume de cathédrale*, at once massive and elusive, there was nostalgia in every line.

" They bear the same name as the Cathedral," the Bishop replied: " St. Dorothy."

Mrs. Shamefoot touched the episcopal sleeve.

" And that calm wee door? " she asked.

" It's the side way in."

" Tell me, Doctor Pantry, is there a ray of hope? "

" Without seeming uncharitable, or unsympathetic, or inhuman, what am I to say? With a little squeezing we might bury you in the precincts of the Cathedral."

" But I don't want to be trodden on."

" You might do a great deal worse than lay down a brass."

" With my head on a cushion and my feet upon flowers. Oh! "

" Or a nice shroud one. Nothing looks better. And they are quite simple to keep clean."

" But a brass," she said, " would lead to rubbings. I know so well! Persons on all fours, perpetually bending over me."

" I can see no objection in that."

" I don't think my husband would like it."

" Naturally; if Mr. Shamefoot would mind——"

" Mind? " She began to titter. " Poor Soco," she said; " poor, dear man. But a window's more respectable. Though I'd sooner I didn't borrow an old one."

And with an effort she manœuvred her hat through the narrow monastic door.

Darkness, and an aroma of fresh lilies, welcomed her, as though with cool, invisible hands.

Here, most likely, would she dwell until the last day surprised her. And, like twelve servants, the hours would bring her moods.

She sank impulsively to her knees. A window like a vast sapphire—a sumptuous sapphire, changing back —chilled her slightly.

Must colour change?

Here and there the glass had become incoherent a little, and begun to mumble.

" One could look for ever at the pretty windows! " she murmured, rising.

The Bishop seemed touched.

" We must try and find you a corner," he said, " somewhere."

She turned towards him.

" Oh, you make me happy."

" I said a corner," the Bishop replied. " Perhaps we can find you a lancet."

" A lancet! But I should be so congested, shouldn't I? I shall need some space. A wee wheel-window, or something of the kind."

The tones implied the colossal.

" A lancet would be rather limited, of course, but does that matter? "

" Wait till you see the designs."

With a sensation of uneasiness Doctor Pantry began to pivot about the font.

" In Cromwell's time," he explained, " it was used as a simple washtub."

" Oh, what a shame! "

" And from here," he said, " you get such a curious complication of arches."

Around the pillars drooped stone garlands that had been coloured once. From them a few torn and marvellous flags, that looked more as if they had waved triumphant over some field of scandal than anywhere else, reposed reminiscent.

" What shreds! "

" Certainly, they are very much riddled."

But she lingered apart a moment before the tomb of an Ashringford maiden, lying sleep-locked upon a pyre of roses, with supplicating angels at the head and feet.

" Do I," she whispered, " detect romance? "

The Bishop bent his head.

" Alas," he said, " the entire *bibliothèque rose.*"

" And how sweet something smells."

" Many persons have noticed it. Even when there has been barely a dry leaf within doors."

" Why, what? "

" It emanates from the Coronna Chapel, where Mrs. Cresswell is."

" Is it there always? "

" It varies. On some days it's as delicate as a single cowslip. On others it's quite strong, more like syringa."

Mrs. Shamefoot scanned the shadows.

" But Mrs. Cresswell," she inquired, " who was she—exactly? "

" Primarily," the Bishop replied, " she was a governess. And with some excellent people too. Apart from which, no doubt, she would have been canonised, but for an unfortunate remark. It comes in in *The Red Rose of Martyrdom.* ' If we are all a part of God,' she says, 'then God must *indeed* be horrible.' "

"Nerves are accountable for a lot. Possibly, her pupils were tiresome. . . . Or it was upon a hot day. In her *Autobiography* she confesses, doesn't she, to her sensibility to heat?"

Doctor Pantry smiled.

"What a charming book!"

"I love it too. It's a book that I adore."

"I have the 1540 edition."

"Have you? how rare!"

"Indeed, it's a possession that I prize."

"I should say so. I can repeat, almost by heart, the chapter that commences: ' What can be more melancholy than Stonehenge at sunset.' Her cry of astonishment on beholding it from the window of Lord Ismore's coach is the earliest impressionary criticism that we have. She was asleep, wasn't she, when a sudden jolt awoke her. ' The stones,' she said, to little Miss Ismore, whom she was piloting to Court, ' the stones are like immense sarcophagi suspended in the air. . . .' "

"Admirable!" the Bishop exclaimed.

"And Miss Ismore in her way was interesting too. Eventually she married Prince Schara, and retired to Russia with him. And kept a diary. Each night she would write down the common-places of the Czarina, with the intention of one day revealing them in a book; as if she hadn't sufficient incidents without! Before her death, in Moscow, where she was poisoned, one gathers that the influences of childhood, although most likely smothered, were not entirely put out. And she would wear her heavenly tiara at the opera as if it were a garland of thorns. Really, the Princess was one of the very first persons to get Russiaphobia."

"Russiaphobia; what is that?"

"Wearing one's rubies and emeralds at the same time," Mrs. Shamefoot said in a hushed voice.

The Bishop waved aside a hanging.

"There is usually," he explained, " a slight charge

asked for entrance to the Coronna Chapel. But to-day you're with me! "

She stood awed.

" How seductive she is; though, somehow, I should call her inclined to be too rotund for a saint! A saint should be slim and flexible as a bulrush. . . ."

" The effect, no doubt, of her fine gaiety! Her exuberance was wonderful. She was as gay as a patch of poppies to the last."

" I suppose, in her time, there were a few flower faces, but the majority of persons seem to have been quite appallingly coarse."

" It has often been remarked that she resembles Madame de Warens. . . ."

Mrs. Shamefoot became regretful.

" If only Rembrandt might have painted Madame de Warens! " she said.

" You have not yet been to our small gallery in the town? "

" I didn't know there was one."

" Oh, but you must go——"

" I will, but not before my own affair's arranged! Wait; a lancet, did you say? Or a wheel-window, or a chancel-light—I'll be confused."

" Before I can make any definite promises," the Bishop said, " an unworthy world is sure to demand a few credentials."

" Dear Doctor Pantry, were I to proclaim myself a saint you'd probably not believe it——"

" Indeed, I assure you I've no misgivings."

" I cannot conceive why, then, there should be any fuss."

" You have never yet come across our *Parish Magazine?* "

" I dare say if I stayed here long enough I'd get horrid too."

" No; I don't think you ever would."

" I might! "

" I assure you every time it appears I find myself wishing I were lying in the sanctity of my own sarcophagus."

"Dear Doctor Pantry, don't say such shocking things! I will not allow it. Besides, I could compose the notice myself."

" Indeed, I fear you'd have to."

" Behind a white mask and a dark cloak. Quite in the manner of Longhi. Thus: ' The beautiful Mrs. S., who (for the next few weeks) wishes to remain unknown, desires to remove from St. Dorothy one of those white windows (which resemble prose), and replace it by,' etc., etc., etc. Or, to slip away the west window altogether. . . ."

" But the west window . . . the pre-Raphaelite window. . . ."

" It's a blot to the Cathedral. I cannot make out what is written beneath; but isn't it to say that in the end the king marries the kitchenmaid and they lived happily ever after? "

"To remove the west window," the Bishop said, " when everyone is alive that subscribed for it, I fear would be impossible."

Mrs. Shamefoot peered about her. Once only, long ago, in the Pyrenees, could she recall a similar absence of accommodation.

" Perhaps," she said half shyly, " I might share the Coronna."

" Share the Coronna! "

Doctor Pantry turned pale at the impiety.

" Why not? Two triangles when they cut can make a star. . . ."

" I fear your Niccolo in Ashringford might be unapprehended."

"After all, what is the Dorothy window but a wonderful splash of colour? "

"Have you tried the Abbey? " Doctor Pantry asked.

" What, Westminster? "

" With a husband in the Cabinet. . . ."

Mrs. Shamefoot smiled sedately.

" But I'm not a public person," she said. " An actress. Although, of course, I do sell flowers."

" With such an object in view, Heaven forfend you should become one."

Mrs. Shamefoot closed her eyes.

" To be an actress," she said; " to ruin one's life before a room full of people. . . . What fun! "

" Every good preacher," Doctor Pantry observed, " has a dash of the comedian too."

" Do you go often to the play? "

" The last time I went," his lordship confessed, " was to see Mrs. Kendall in *The Elder Miss Blossom*."

" Oh, she's perfect."

" Although Lady Anne saw Yvette Guilbert only the other day."

Mrs. Shamefoot looked sympathetic.

" I can imagine nothing more sinister," she said, " than Yvette Guilbert singing ' Where-are-you-going-to-my-pretty-maid.' It will haunt me always." And she paused meditatively to admire a stone effigy of the first Lady Blueharnis, stretched out upon a pillow like a dead swan.

" How entirely charming the memorials are."

" I'm so glad that you like them."

" Somehow, some people are so utterly of this world," she mused, " that one cannot conceive of them being grafted into any other."

But a sound of unselfconscious respiration from behind the Blueharnis monument startled her.

" Macabre person! . . . Fiend! " she said.

Winsome looked up sleepily.

" I came," he explained, " to collect a few books for Mrs. Henedge."

Mrs. Shamefoot blinked.

" That looks," she observed, " like going."

" I don't want to be too hard on her," the Bishop said, " but I think she might have told me first."

" I cannot say," Winsome said. " In the country one is always grateful to find anything to do."

" Have you been here long? "

" Since yesterday. Already I could howl for staleness."

Mrs. Shamefoot glanced at the Bishop.

" Very likely," she said; " but to run away the moment you arrive, just because it's the most appealing place on earth . . . I should call it decadent! "

And, indeed, after a few hours nearer Nature, perpetually it was the same with him. A *nostalgie du pavé* began to set in. He would miss the confidential " Things is very bad, sir," of the newspaper boy at the corner; the lights, the twinkling advertisements of the Artistic Theatre . . . the crack of the revolver so audible those nights that the heroine killed herself, the suspense, the subsequent sickening silence; while the interest, on lighter evenings, would be varied by the " Call me my biplane," of Indignation as it flew hurriedly away.

Mrs. Shamefoot picked up a rich red-topped hymnbook.

" And so," she said, " the aloe, apparently, has bloomed! "

" No; not yet. But there's nothing like being ready."

" And when do you think it's to be? "

" I hardly care to say. Though, when the change is made, you can be certain it will be done quite quietly."

" In Ashringford," the Bishop said, " nothing is ever done quite quietly."

" But that's so silly of Ashringford! " Mrs. Shamefoot exclaimed. " When my sister 'verted, I assure you nobody took the slightest notice. But then, of course, she was always going backwards and forwards. . . . She made excursions into three different religions. And she always came back dissatisfied and grumbling."

"The world is disgracefully managed, one hardly knows to whom to complain."

"Many people," the Bishop remarked, "are very easily influenced. They have only to look at a peacock's tail to think of Brahma."

Mrs. Shamefoot turned her eyes towards the entrancing glass.

How mysterious it was! Like the luminous carpets that veil a dream.

She became abstracted a moment, lost in mental measurements, unhappy and elaborate-looking, in her mourning, as a wasted columbine.

"Well, since you're here, Mr. Brookes," she said, "you must absolutely try the organ. And Doctor Pantry has never heard me sing."

XI

FROM a choice of vivid cushions she placed the least likely behind her head.

"I'm ready!" And with a tired, distrustful smile she looked away towards the house as if it were a hospital.

At her feet crouched an animal who, hourly, was assuming an expression as becoming, and as interesting, she believed, as the wolf of St. Francis. Her hands full of dark clematis, clutched and crowned. . . .

"There'll be the funnel of the jam factory, and a few chimney-pots for background," Winsome said. "Do you mind?"

"My dear, what can I do? In the end, these horrid encroaching shapes will drive me out."

"One, two, three; do smile . . . less. I'd rather work a water-wheel than be a photographer."

Mrs. Henedge relaxed.

"I wish," she murmured, "instead, you'd decide about being Rose."

"I will. But in these wilds the very notion of a début makes one shiver."

"My dear Mr. Brookes, when you give your first concert I will lead you on to the platform and stay by you all the time!"

"Well, I'm vacillating. I only need a push."

"Oh, be careful of the tail."

And, indeed, an animal who had bitten a poet, worried a politician, amused a famous actress and harried a dancer was not to be ignored.

How was it possible, it may be asked, for anything in Ashringford to have come in contact with such celebrities? By what accident had these Illustrious crossed his path? Incidentally, St. Dorothy was responsible for all.

And now that Miss Compostella was awaited at Stockingham, and with a Rose de Tivoli within reach, there appeared every likelihood of lengthening the list—a poet, a politician, a pianist, *two* famous actresses, etc., in anticipation—he counted them over upon his paws, surveying, meanwhile, the newly planted scene; for his lady cared only for those airier sorts of trees, larches, poplars, willows, so that, in the spring, the garden looked extraordinarily inexperienced and green.

" I shall have to chloroform him," Mrs. Henedge said, " if he does it again."

" He might be grateful. One can never tell."

" Why, what's wrong? "

" I've so many moods. You cannot like 'em all. . . . I'm never characteristic! "

" Poor Mr. Vane! Never mind if you're bored. Relax! Recoup! The country's very good for you."

" That's what everyone says. Mrs. Shamefoot said the same to me this morning."

" Oh, have you seen her? "

" In the Cathedral. Do you know, if I stopped here long, I'd start a Satanic colony in your midst just to share the monotony."

" My dear, there's one already."

" Direct me——"

" No; stay here and be good. I've something to tell you that will please you."

" Me? "

" Yes. Old Mrs. Felix said to my maid: ' I think Mr. Brookes so beautiful. He has such a young, romantic face! ' "

" What else did she say? "

" She said nothing more."

" Hooray! "

Mrs. Henedge raised a finger. " S-S-Sh! or you'll disturb Monsignor Parr. He's half asleep in a rocking-chair making his soul."

" According to Monsignor Parr, heaven will be a perpetual concert. Do you think that true? "

" I believe he has been *favoured*. . . . In fact, in the little powdering closet, before it became my oratory, something picked him up, and danced him round. . . ."

" Oh! When? "

" Only the other day. My dear, yes! And *twice* in the month of Mary! "

" Zoom—zoom! "

" Read to me."

" What shall I read? "

" Get the Lascelles Abercrombie, or the Francis Jammes——"

" ' La maison serait pleine de roses et de guêpes ' —that's adorable."

" It makes one dormitive too."

" Let's talk of it."

She sighed shortly.

" With so many tiresome cats about, it ought to be protected."

" Still, with a bronze-green door at night and a violet curtain in the day——"

" I know! "

" And what is it to be? "

" I suppose we shall adhere to the original plan, after all, and call it John the Baptist."

" Oh, don't! "

" And why not, pray? "

" For lack of humour," Winsome said, " I know of nothing in the world to compare with the Prophet's music in *Salomé*. It's the quintessence of villadom. It suggests the Salvation Army, and General Booth. It——"

" You don't like it? " she interrupted him.

" Not very much."

" If you're going to be childish, I propose you should take a walk."

" There is nowhere attractive to go."

" My dear, there are the walls. They are not Roman walls, but they are very nice walls."

" I find it rather boring, the merely picturesque."

" Then I'm sure I hardly know——"

" I've an irresistible inclination to attend Mrs. Featherstonehaugh's fête in the Close—*admittance a shilling.*"

" Keep your money, my dear boy, or look through the fence."

" Ah, Rome! . . ."

" Well, I'm going indoors. I've letters. . . . Perhaps you want to write to Andrew, too? I expect he must miss you."

" Poor Andrew! He goes stumbling along towards some ideal; it's difficult to say quite what."

" The more reason, then, to write to him."

" Oh, stay; another minute, please; and I'll be g-good——"

" Then put your tie straight, my dear Rose. . . . And, *mind Balthasar's tail!* "

XII

" HAIL, angel! "

" Darling! "

" Dearest! "

" I've been thinking about you so much, dear, all day."

" Well, I find myself thinking of you too. . . . "

George Calvally had collided with Miss Thumbler, holding " a marvellous bargain," a score of music and a parasol.

" At the corner of Vigo Street," she confessed, " my *ear* began to burn, so frightfully."

" Are you going anywhere, dear? "

" I was in the act," she said, shivering, and growing strangely spiritual, " of paying a little bill."

" Then—— "

He looked up. Overhead the sky was so pale that it appeared to have been powdered completely with *poudre-de-riz*.

" The proper place," he said, " to feel the first hint of autumn, I always think, is the angle of Regent Street, close to the Piccadilly Hotel."

" How splendidly sequestered, dear, it sounds! "

And already, quite perceptibly, there was a touch of autumn in the air.

In the shops the chrysanthemums mingled with the golden leaves of beech. Baskets of rough green pears lay smothered beneath blue heather.

" How sweet, child, you look! "

" I'm so glad. Have I changed since yesterday? Sunday in town leaves such scars. . . . Have I my profile still? "

" You've got it. Juſt! " he assured her.

For the dread of Miss Thumbler's life was that one day she should find herself without it.

" And do you like me, deareſt, so? Mamma considers me quite ghaſtly in *crêpe;* she seems to fancy it may somehow cause an earthquake in Cremona, and bring down a doom upon papa. . . ."

" You're wonderful. You should never, never wear anything else."

" And it's scarcely a second since I commanded a muslin sprinkled with showers of tiny multi-coloured spots like handfuls of confetti flung all over it! "

" Darling! "

" Deareſt! "

Now that George Calvally had lifted Mira up into the sun, she had become more melodious perhaps.

Continually she would be tying things round her forehead, to her mother's absolute aſtonishment, or perusing, diligently, the lives of such charaĉters as Saskia, Heléne Fourment, Mrs. Blake. . . .

Sometimes, when the mood seized her, she would wander, for hours, through the slow, deep ſtreets of the capital, in a ſtiff, shelving mantle, with long, unfashionable folds. At other times, too, she would meet George Calvally, swathed like an idol, and they would drive together in a taxi, full of twilight, holding each other's hands. Oh, the mad amusement of Piccadilly . . . the charm, unspeakable, of the Strand . . . the intoxication of the Embankment towards St. Paul's.

" Darling, what would you care to do? "

" At the Coliseum," she said, " they're giving *Georges Dandin,* with the music of Lully. Shall we go?"

He laughed.

" On such a glorious afternoon it would be ungrateful to ſtay indoors."

" But Professor Inglepin, dear, has designed the dresses, and his sense of coſtume is simply . . ."

" Angelic one, he's getting . . ."

" Though, certain busts of Bernini, George——"

" Oh, mind. . . . There's weariness! "

Holding a pink-purple flower to her nose, her eyes closed, Miss Compostella swept by them, in some jewelled hades of her own.

" How magnificent she looked! "

Mira turned, serpentine.

"Was that the first sign of autumn, do you suppose?"

" Listen. I've something to ask you, child."

With her scroll of music she caressed, sympathetically, his arm.

" It's about the church your father's setting up."

" Dearest, he says *it's the last he ever means to build.*"

" Mrs. Henedge has asked me to undertake the frescoes. . . ."

" That's joy! "

" But you must help."

" You mean . . . give me time, dear, I'll see."

" Darling! Decide."

" Wouldn't Rosamund——? "

" Impossible. Every five minutes she needs a rest! Besides——"

" Rubbish, besides! "

" But I need *you.*"

" What will Mary say? "

" What difference can it make to her? "

" I suppose not. She left, just now, the sweetest note, with tickets for the Queen's Hall."

" She's very fond of you, I know."

" Oh, George, it makes me miserable to think of her."

He hailed a taxi.

" How would the Wallace be? "

" The Collection? " he exclaimed. " Isn't it indoors . . . dear! And surely it's the most *stagnant* place on earth? "

XIII

"Wierus, Furiel, Charpon, Charmias!"

The very air seemed charged with tragic thoughts. The play of colour from her aura was so bright it lit the room.

"Charmias!" she called compellingly.

Stretched out upon an Anne settle, watching her, Lady Castleyard lay, in a rather beautiful heap.

"Can you see anything?" she inquired. With a bottle of pact-ink overturned upon the dressing-table, she had retreated to the background, to be "out of the way."

"Selah! . . ."

Lady Castleyard took up a mirror.

"If the devil won't come," she said, "we can't force him."

Mrs. Shamefoot seemed piqued.

"Not come? Why, he's taken all the wave out of my hair."

"It certainly *is* less successful, from the side."

"What would you advise?"

"I should take what the Bishop offers you. Don't break adrift again."

"You'd accept Ashringford?"

"Well. . . . One may as well as not!"

She collapsed, disheartened.

"I'm like a loose leaf," she moaned, "tossed about the world."

"Don't be so foolish; probably it's more amusing for the loose leaf than for the rooted tree."

"And you no longer care to join?"

"Birdie, when I've squared my card losses, and

my race losses, and my dressmaker, and redecorated our new house a little, I'll have nothing over."

" There's Lionel! . . ."

" Oh, he's so prodigal; I know I'll die in a ditch."

" Then it's clear, of course, you mustn't."

" Besides, Biddy, you couldn't expect me to climb away into the tracery lights; it would be like singing Souzouki in *Butterfly*."

" And you forgive me? "

" I bear no bitterness."

Mrs. Shamefoot moved towards the window.

The gardens looked almost heroic in the evening light. If the statues, that lit the sombre evergreens of the walks, did *not* suggest Phidias, they did, at least, their duty.

" When the birds fly low, and the insects turn, and turn," she said, " there's rain! "

Lady Castleyard closed her eyes.

" I like a storm," she murmured, " particularly at night. Sometimes one can catch a face in it—somebody one's been wondering about, perhaps, or who's been wondering of you. And one meets in the explosion."

With a string of pearls Mrs. Shamefoot flicked at a passing bat.

" We should dress," she observed, " for dinner."

" Sir Isaac is strolling about outside still, isn't he? "

Mrs. Shamefoot peered out.

Already the sun had dipped below the hills, using, above Ashringford, the golds and purples of Poussin that suggested Rome. In the twilight the old, partly disused, stables looked strangely mysterious and aloof.

" And Sir Isaac? "

" Yes, he's there still; like a tourist without a guide-book. But he's not going to be stitched into a Poiret model by eight; nor has his head been ruffled recently by the devil."

"Is that a Poiret shimmering across the bed? . . . What does Soco say?"

"My dear, he never looks. In the spring he goes striding past the first violet; and it's always the same."

"I wish he'd take up Lionel until my ball-room's done. His idea of decoration never varies, and it's becoming so wearisome. Horns at intervals! . . ."

"How appalling!"

"We shall be all spears and antlers when you come."

"Have you that same artistic footman still?"

"Oh, heavens; yes!"

"I adored him. He would clap his hand to his forehead whenever he forgot the . . . potatoes in an attitude altogether *Age d'Airain*."

"Biddy, see who it is; there's somebody at the door."

"It's me!"

"Who's me?"

"It's Sumph."

"Who's Sumph?"

"It's me."

"I know."

"I'm Miss Compostella's maid."

"So Julia's *here*."

"Opst!"

"And when did she arrive?"

Sumph smiled. "I've been buzzing about the house," she said, "this last *half*-hour."

"Indeed!"

"Miss Compostella sent me downstairs after a cucumber. Travelling disorients her so. And I must have missed my way."

"I believe she's in the Round Tower."

"The housekeeper did say. But had she been the mother of Roxolana, Duchess of Dublin, she could hardly have been more brief."

Mrs. Shamefoot became concerned.

"When you find your way again," she said, "give your mistress these, with my love; they're certain to cure her."

"The poor soul was stretched out like some dead thing that breathes," Sumph murmured, "as I came away."

Nevertheless, at dinner, nobody could have guessed Miss Compostella's recent critical condition. Had she returned that moment from a month at Mürren one would have wondered still what she had employed.

"It's only now and then," she informed Lord Blueharnis, inclining towards him, "that I ever venture; wine has to be utterly exquisite, or I make a face!"

Falling between Dean Manly and Mr. Guy Fox, she resembled a piece of Venice glass between two strong schoolroom mugs.

"I expect he'll fall in love some day with somebody," Lady Georgia exclaimed, injuring a silence, "and marry; or don't you think he will?"

"Marry; who?"

"Claud Harvester."

"Why should he? If Claud can be the Gaby Deslys of literature now, he doesn't seem to mind."

"But would he be literature?"

"Why, of course!"

"*Love's Arrears*," Dean Manly said, "was an amazing piece of work."

Miss Compostella turned upon him.

"I'm Maggie!" she said.

But Mrs. Shamefoot took compassion upon the Dean's surprise.

"He's become almost *too* doll-like and *Dorothy* latterly," she inquired, "hasn't he?"

"Of course, Claud's considered a cult, but everybody reads him!"

"And Mr. Garsaint's comedy?"

" With the exception of Maria Random, Anna's maid, the cast is quite complete."

" I suppose Anna Comnena had a maid? " Mr. Guy Fox remarked.

Lady Georgia stiffened a candle that had begun to bend.

" I want you to tell me, presently," she said, "about young Chalmers. I used to know his mother long ago. She was a great hypocrite, poor dear, but I was very fond of her, all the same! "

But Miss Compostella never put off anything.

" Oh, well," she said, " of course he's wonderfully good-looking and gifted, and rather a draw; but I dislike playing with him. Directly he comes on to the stage he begins to perspire."

" And that nice little Mr. Williams? "

" *He* joined the Persian Ballet."

Mrs. Guy Fox put up her lorgnon. Her examination of the purple Sèvres dessert service and the James I spoons, she intended, should last at least two minutes; her aversion to the word *perspire* was only equalled by her horror of the word *flea*. . . .

And indeed Mrs. Guy Fox was continually upon the alert.

Ever since her sisters-in-law had been carried off by peers, she had looked upon her husband as a confirmed stick-in-the-mud. It was unreasonable of her, Mr. Guy Fox complained, when it was hardly to be hoped that Fortune would repeat herself with him.

" No, really, I ask for nothing better," Mrs. Shamefoot said to the Dean, " than to waste my sweetness on the desert air. . . ."

" And I see no reason why you should not," he replied. " The Bishop, I'm confident, doesn't intend to be disobliging."

" Yes; but you know he is! "

" I wish it were in my power to be of service to

you. But you're negotiating, I believe, with five or six cathedrals, at the present time?"

"Not so many. I've Overcares in view, though to be surrounded by that unpleasant Gala glass would be a continual strain. And then, there's Carnage. But somehow the East Coast never appealed to me. It's so stringy."

"Even Ely?" he inquired.

"Oh, Ely's beautiful. But how sad!"

"Ashringford, also, is sad. Sometimes, in winter, the clouds fall right down upon us. And the towers of St. Dorothy remain lost in them for days."

"A *mariage mystique* would be just what I'd enjoy."

"Has it occurred to you to become identified with some small, some charming church, the surprisal of which, in an obscure alley, would amount almost to an adventure?"

"But I'm so tired," she said, "of playing Bo-Peep."

"Still, some cosy gem!"

"A cosy gem?"

"St. Lazarus, for instance——"

"I'm told it leaks. There are forty-two holes in the roof."

"Or St. Anastasia."

"St. Anastasia is quite unsafe. Besides, I can't endure a spire. It's such a slope."

"St. Mary Magdalen?" he ventured.

"I have her life upstairs! Did you know she was actually engaged to John the Baptist? Until Salome *broke it off.* It was only after the sad affair at the palace that Mary really buckled to and became what she afterwards became. But her church here is so pitch dark, and it's built, throughout, with flints. I couldn't bear it."

"Or Great St. Helen's!"

She shuddered.

"There's the graveyard," she said. "I'd never like

118

it. I don't understand the tombs. And I hope I never shall! Those urns with towels thrown over them cast shades like thirteenth-century women."

"It's unaccountable to me," the Dean said, "that you should care to tie yourself to consecrated ground, when you might be an Independent. A Theodoric!"

"I hope you'll make it plain to Doctor Pantry," Lady Georgia said to him, as the ladies left the room, "that she's fading fast away. She has scarcely tumbled a crumb between her lips now for weeks. It almost breaks my heart to look at her."

Miss Compostella twined an arm about her friend.

"If *I* worship anything," she confessed, "it's trees. . . ."

"Come outside; the flowers smell so sweet in the dark."

The tired cedars in the park had turned to blackened emerald, the air seemed smeared with bloom. Here and there, upon the incomparably soft grey hills, a light shone like a very clear star.

"How admirable. 'Orgy,' it is!"

"Though to my idea," Lady Georgia said, "the hills would undoubtedly gain if some sorrowful creature could be induced to take to them. I often long for a bent, slim figure, to trail slowly along the ridge, at sundown, in an agony of regret."

Mrs. Guy Fox drew on a glove.

"I'm quite certain," she remarked, "that Lord Blueharnis would not require much pressing."

Lady Georgia made her gentlest grimace.

"I wish," she said, "he would, for his figure's sake. He is getting exactly like that awkward effigy of the late Earl in the Public Gardens."

"Mrs. Barrow of Dawn vows she can fall in love with it a mile away."

"Poor Violet! Cooped up half the year with an old man and seven staid servants, it cannot be very gay."

" They say if she's absent, even an hour together," Mrs. Guy Fox said, " he sends a search party after her. And he's so miserably mean. Why, the collar of pearls he gave his first wife strangled her! "

" I heard she died in torment; but I didn't know from what."

Mrs. Shamefoot held the filmy feathers of her fan slantwise across the night. It pleased her to watch whole planets gleam between the fragile sticks.

"Nobody," she exclaimed, "would do for me the things that I would do for them! "

". . . One can never be sure *what* a person will do unless one has tried."

Lady Georgia drew a scarf devotionally about her head.

" Julia has offered to speak some scenes from tragedies to us," she said.

" Gladly, Georgia, I will, when we're full numbers."

" Here come our husbands now! "

" At the risk of seeming sentimental," Sir Isaac declared, " I want to tell you how good your dinner was; it was excellent."

" All millionaires love a baked apple," Lady Georgia murmured, as she led the way with him towards the Greek theatre.

" ' Que ton âme est bien née Fille d'Agamemnon,' " Miss Compostella declaimed dispassionately, by way of tuning up.

In sympathetic silence Mrs. Shamefoot followed with the Dean.

The statues stood like towers above the low dwarf trees, dark, now, against the night. Across the gardens, from the town, the Cathedral bells chimed ten. Ten silver strokes, like the petals falling from a rose.

She sighed. She sought support. She swayed. . . .

XIV

ALAS, that conviviality should need excuse!

While Miss Compostella, somewhat tardily, raised the Keen for Iphigenia, Lady Anne conducted a dinner conference, for women alone.

A less hospitable nature, no doubt, would have managed (quite charmingly) upon tea. But Lady Anne scorned the trickle.

Nor was it before the invitations were consigned to the pillar-box in the Palace wall that she decided, in deference to the Bishop, who was in Sintrap, to add the disarming nuance. To append which, with a hair-pin, she had forced the postman's lock.

For indeed excess is usually the grandparent to deceit. And now, with a calm mind beneath a small tiara, she leaned an elbow, conferentially, upon a table decorated altogether recklessly by Aurelia, with acacia-leaves and apostle spoons.

She had scarcely set her spark.

" No, really! . . . I can't think *why* she should have it," Miss Wardle exclaimed, leaping instantly into a blaze.

" She's very handsome, isn't she? And that's always something. And when you're next in Sloane Street you'll observe she has a certain wayward taste for arranging flowers."

" If those are her chief credentials, I shall not interfere. . . ."

" Nobody denies her her taste for flowers," Mrs. Pontypool exclaimed. " Though, from her manner of dress, one wouldn't perhaps take her to be a Christian. But handsome! I must say, I don't think so. Such a little pinched, hard, cold, shrivelled face. With a profile like the shadow of a doubt. And with a phantom husband too, whom nobody has ever seen."

" To be fair to her, one has read his ridiculous speeches."

" If a window is allowed at all, surely Miss Brice should have it? "

" But why should the Cathedral be touched? It's far too light as it is. Often, I assure you, we all of us look quite old. . . . The sun streams in on one in such a manner."

" Besides, when she has already nibbled at Perch, why must she come to us? "

" Nibbled! One fancies her to have stormed Over-cares, Carnage, Sintrap, Whetstone, Cowby, Mawling, Marrow and Marrowby, besides beseeching Perch."

" If she could only bring herself to wait," Mrs. Wookie wailed, " Mrs. Henedge might cater for her at St. John's. . . ."

" St. John's! From what one hears, it will be a perfect Mosque."

Lady Anne refused a peach.

" I've begged the Dean to propose something smaller to her," she said, "than St. Dorothy, where she can put up a window and be as whimsical as she likes."

" That's common-sense. It wouldn't matter much what she did at Crawbery."

" Or even in the town. So many of the smaller churches are falling into dilapidation. It's quite sad. Only this evening Miss Critchett was complaining bitterly of the draught at St. Mary's. Her life, she says, is one ceaseless cold. A window there, that would shut, would be such a blessing."

" And the building, I believe, is distinctly Norman."

" Call it Byzantine to her. . . ."

" It's a pity she won't do something useful with her money. Repair a clock that wanders, for instance, or pension off some bells. Whenever those bells near us begin to ring they sound such bargains."

" Or fence in St. Cyriac, where my poor Percy is," Mrs. Wookie said pathetically. " It really isn't nice the way the cows get in and loll among the tombs. If it's only for the milk——"

" What is your vote, Mrs. Pontypool? "

" Oh, my dear, don't ask me! I mean to be passive. I mean to be neutral. I shan't interfere."

" But isn't it one's duty? "

" Well, I'm always glad of any change," Mrs. Barrow said. " Any little brightness. Nothing ever happens here."

Miss Wookie became clairvoyant. " If I'm not much mistaken," she said, " it's an expiatory window she intends us to admire."

" That's perfectly possible."

" Indeed, it's more than likely."

" For some imprudence, perhaps. Some foolish step. . . ."

" Ah, poor thing . . .! "

" And in any case the window, for her, will be a kind of osprey! "

" One could understand a window in moderation, but apparently she's quite insatiable."

" When my hour comes," Mrs. Wookie said, " I shall hope to lie in the dear kitchen-garden."

Miss Wardle groped about her, and shivered slightly.

" I'd like my cloak," she murmured, " please, if you don't mind."

And indeed it was a matter of surprise, and a sign of success, that she had not sent for it before.

For any gathering that might detain her beyond her own gate after dark it was her plan to assume a cloak of gold galloon that had hidden, once, the shoulders of the Infanta Maria Isabella.

123

How the garment had reached Miss Wardle's wardrobe was unknown; but that she did not disown it was clear, since frequently she would send a footman for it midway during dinner. It was like the whistle that sounded half-time at a football match, bucolic neighbours said.

"What is the feeling about it in the town?" Lady Anne inquired.

"Until the decision is final, people hardly know which way to object. But Mr. Dyce says if she has the window, he'll show up the Cathedral."

"Really! Horrid old man! What can he mean?"

"Insolency!"

"And Mr. Pet. . . . But, my dear, fortunately he's such a rapid preacher. One misses half he says."

"The text he took on Sunday was Self-Idolatry, the Golden Calf. . . ."

"I thought it was to be green!"

"What, the calf?"

"No, the window."

"Perhaps he'll go before it's all arranged."

"Very likely. I hear he finds Ashringford so expensive. . . ."

Mrs. Pontypool scratched her smooth fair fringe.

"I suppose," she said, "poor young man, with exactly twopence a year, he'd find everywhere ruinous."

"And then, I wonder, who will take his place?"

"Oh, surely Mr. Olney will."

"He's such a boy. . . ."

"My dear, age is no obstacle. And his maiden sermon came as a complete surprise! Of course, he was a trifle nervous. He shook in his shoes till his teeth rattled. And his hair stood on end. But, all the same, he was very brilliant."

"Oh, don't!" Miss Pontypool murmured.

And indeed, notwithstanding a certain analogy between her home circle with that of the Cenci, she

was almost an Ingenious. She would say " Don't! "
" Oh, don't! " " My dear, don't! " apropos of nothing
at all.

" Oh, don't! " she murmured.

" I recall a song of his about a kangaroo," Mrs.
Wookie said, " once. At a hunt ball."

" Garoo-garoo-garoo, wasn't it? " Aurelia asked.
" Disgraceful."

" My dear, *don't*. . . ."

" How fortunate for that little Miss Farthing if he
should come. Although she'd have to change her
ways. As I've so often tried to tell her, one should
wear tailor-mades in the country, instead of going
about like a manicure on her holiday."

" I don't believe there is anything in that," Miss
Hospice said.

" I'm not at all sure. Whenever they meet he gives
such funny little gasps. . . ."

" Mr. Olney needs a wife who could pay *at least* her
own expenses."

" What has he a year? "

" He owns to a thousand. But he has quite fifteen
hundred."

" Besides, he's too pale, and his face lacks purpose."

Lady Anne rapped her fan with pathos.

" Any side issues," she said, " might be settled
later."

" Well, I don't see why she should have it," Miss
Wardle repeated. " To the glory of Mrs. Shamefoot,
and of the Almighty. . . . No, really I can't see
why! "

" Had she been a saint," Mrs. Wookie observed,
" it would have been another matter."

" There's not much, my dear, to choose between
women. Things are done on a different scale. That's
all."

" Hush, Aurelia! How can you be such a cynic! "

" All the same," Miss Pantry said, " trotting to the Cathedral solely of a Sunday, and caring about oneself, solely, all the week, is like crawling into heaven by weekly instalments. . . ."

" Indeed, that's charitable," Miss Chimney, who was dining at the Palace as a " silent protest," was constrained to say.

" But it's such a commonplace thing to do, to condemn a person one knows next to nothing of! "

" Mrs. Shamefoot was at St. Dorothy, for the Thanksgiving, wasn't she? "

" I believe so. But Miss Middling sat immediately before me. And with all that yellow wheat in her hat I couldn't see a thing."

" I remarked her rouging her lips very busily during a long Amen."

" Well, I couldn't quite make out what she had on. But she looked very foreign from behind."

" That was Lady Castleyard. Mrs. Shamefoot's little jacket was plainer than any cerecloth. And on her head there was the saddest slouch. . . ."

" Then she shall have my vote. For counting the pin-holes in it made me positively dizzy."

" And you may add mine."

" And mine. . . ."

" I forbid anything of the kind, Kate," her mother said. " Lady Anne will return it me, I'm sure." And extending a withered hand in the direction of the vote she slipped some salted almonds into her bosom.

" Oh, Tatty! "

" I shall put your vote with mine, Kate," she said, " for it grieves me to see you are such an arrant fool."

" Don't! "

" Where's the good of stirring up Karma for nothing? " Aurelia wondered.

Mrs. Barrow shook her head sceptically.

" I've too little confidence," she said, " in straws

and smoke, as it is, to credit the pin-marks of a bonnet. It was her maid's."

" How agnostic, Violet, you are! I shall have you going over to Mrs. Henedge before you've done."

" Why, she wears the Cathedral even now."

" I thought she had dropped it. She is getting so tawdry."

" There's a powder-puff and a bottle of Jordan water, or Eau Jeunesse, of hers here still," Aurelia said. "*Besides* a blotting-book."

" I'm not surprised. She appears to have entirely lost her head. The last time I called upon her, the cards *In* and *Out*, on the hall table, were both equally in evidence."

" It's safer to keep away from her," Mrs. Wookie murmured. " I've maintained it all along."

" No doubt, in our time, most of us have flirted with Rome," Mrs. Pontypool remarked, " but, poor dear, she never knew where to stop."

Lady Anne accepted a conferential cigarette from Mrs. Barrow of Dawn.

" Since the affair appears a decided deadlock," she pronounced, " I move that we adjourn."

Miss Valley manœuvred, slightly, her chair.

" I'm so eager to examine those Mortlake tapestries of Mrs. Cresswell," she said, " if they're not away on loan."

" They're on the Ponte di Sospiri," Lady Anne replied, " that connects us to the cloisters. But at night, I fear, it's usually rather dark."

" Impressions I adore. And there's quite a useful little moon."

Aurelia appeared amused.

" Even with a young moon," she said, " like a broken banana, and Lady Anne's crown, and my carved celluloid combs, and all the phosphorescent beetles there may be (and there are), trooping in beastly battalions through the corridors of the Palace, and the fireflies in the garden, and the flickerings in the cemetery, and, indeed, the entire infinity of stars besides, without a little artificial light of our own, one might just as well stop here."

Lady Anne looked at her.

"Don't be so ridiculous, my dear, but lead the way!"

"If the electric isn't in repair I refuse to stir."

"I'm taking the Historian to inspect some curtains," Lady Anne announced, "if anyone would care to come."

"Historian? . . ."

Mrs. Pontypool revealed her Orders.

Quite perceptibly she became the patroness of seven hospitals, two convalescent homes, with shares in a *maison de santé*.

"We must have a little chat," she exclaimed, "together, you and I! All my own family had talent. Only, money, alas, came between them and it."

"My dear, don't!"

"Indeed, it was getting on for genius. And even still my brother (her uncle) will sometimes sit down and write the most unwinking lies. Of course, novels——"

Miss Wardle fastened her cape.

"I should hate to prostitute myself," she remarked, "for *six* shillings."

"Or for four and sixpence cash. . . ."

"Some people publish their works at a guinea," Miss Valley murmured, as she followed Lady Anne towards the door.

The Ponte di Sospiri, whither Lady Anne advanced —built by a previous bishop, to symbolise a perpetual rainbow—broke, quite unexpectedly, from the stairs with all the freedom of a polonaise.

Behind their hostess the ladies trooped, as if Miss

Pantry's timely warning had made it imperative to wade. The concern, indeed, of Mrs. Barrow was such that it caused a blushing butler to retreat.

" My dear Violet! " Lady Anne began, " the only time, I believe, I ever——"

But Mrs. Wookie intervened.

" There is somebody," she remarked, " thumping at the gate."

" It is probably only the post."

And turning to the tapestries Lady Anne commenced the inspection, starting instinctively at the end. And the end, as she pointed out, was simply frantic Bacchanals. After (*à rebours*) came the Martyrdom, spoken often of as " I've had such a busy morning!", the saints' final word. A model, in every particular, of what a martyrdom should be. And indeed nothing could have been simpler, quieter, or better done. There was no squeezing, fainting, crushing or tramping. No prodding. . . . The spectators, provided, each, with a couch and a cup of chocolate, were there by invitation alone. Although, in the market-place (as one might see), tickets were being disposed of at a price. And in the centre of all stood Mrs. Cresswell, leaning with indifference upon a crosier, inset with a humorous and a somewhat scathing eye.

And so, in the dim light, the fourteen panels ran: growing, as they receded, less and less serene, until, at the opening scene, the atmosphere was one of positive gloom.

" It was the ' Marriage.' "

" What do people marry for? " Miss Wardle said. " I've sometimes wondered."

" My dear, don't ask me."

" One marries for latitude, I suppose."

" Or to become a widow."

" I'd give such *worlds* to be a widow," Miss Pontypool declared.

" It's a difficult thing to be," Mrs. Barrow assured her.

" I'm that disgusted with Love," Miss Valley volunteered in her chastest Cockney voice.

" I find it dreadfully disappointin'," Lady Anne supported her.

Mrs. Wookie sighed.

" Mine," she said, " is a nature that cries for more ethereal things."

" Banal passions," Miss Wardle whispered faintly, " fail to stir me."

" ' I'm that disgusted with love,' " the ladies chanted charmingly all together.

" If that is Mr. Cresswell," Mrs. Barrow remarked, " I'm certainly not surprised."

" He's so worn," Miss Chimney observed critically, " and she's so *passée.*"

Aurelia touched the tapestries with her thumb. " It's probably only the stuff."

" And who would this be? " Miss Valley queried, trailing towards an easel with a little quick glide.

" That! " Lady Anne said. " I suppose it was Walter once."

" If I were getting painted," Mrs. Pontypool announced, " again I'd try Mr. White. He doesn't reject beauty. And he reveals the sitter's soul."

Miss Chimney showed some sensitiveness.

" Anything nude, anything undressed, anything without a *frill,*" she said, " revolts me somehow so. I'm sure in the winter, when the trees show their branches—well, I go, when I can, to the South."

But the appearance of the Miss Chalfonts upon the stairs, closely entwined, their eyes astream, their bodies racked by laughter, a single superb boa shared more or less between them, caused a commotion.

" We rang and we rang," Miss Clara said.

" I'm so sorry. But, at all events, you've dined? "

Miss Blanche quite collapsed. "Why, no!" she said.

"Do you abominate almonds?" Mrs. Wookie asked.

Miss Constantia placed a hand before her eyes. "If there's anything on this earth," she said, "I've a horror of, or an aversion for, it's that."

And her gesture seemed to make vibrate all those other objections latent in her too. All those other antipathies, *less* than almonds, that were hereditary, perhaps. She began suddenly to droop. She stood there, dreaming.

"Unwind, can't you," her sister said, "and let me out."

Miss Chalfont commenced to turn.

"It's not from coquetry," she confessed gaily, "that we're last. But the nearer one lives, somehow, the later one's sure to be."

"To be frank," Lady Anne said absently, "you might be stopping in the house."

They were free. . . .

Their garments, the ladies noted, were white and sparkling streaked with green.

Never, Miss Valley affirmed, had she encountered so many charming Ideas. Even at a Poet's dinner.

"Now I know," she said, "exactly where to tie a necklace. On my arm."

"We were getting rather nervous about the vote," Miss Clara said, "so we decided to bring it ourselves. It's the first engagement we've kept for I don't know how long!"

"And which way is it?"

Miss Clara indicated the Cathedral.

"I would read them my essay on Self-Control," Miss Hospice murmured, "if you thought it would have any effect."

"It would probably make them infinitely worse.

It might even kill them outright. And then it would be murder," Miss Valley said.

Miss Hospice smiled sedately.

" My publisher, at any rate, could be found," she said. " I've had the same man always. Byron had him. And Coleridge had him. And Keats. I should be really ashamed to flutter from *firm to firm* like some of those things one sees. . . . I simply couldn't do it. And God looks after me! He has never abandoned me yet to sit up night after night in a public-house to libel His saints by Christmas."

" My dear, I congratulate you! To compose an essay on Self-Control when one is so strangely devoid of it oneself was an admirable *tour de force*."

But the Miss Chalfonts were becoming increasingly unstrung.

" Oh, hold me! " Miss Blanche sighed, sinking, slowly, like the Sienese Santa of the frescoes, to the floor. Miss Clara and Miss Constantia made a movement, which, although a miracle of rhythm, was ineffectual upon the whole.

With quiet complacence Mrs. Wookie took a chair.

" They're off! " she said.

" If Lord Chesterfield could only see them now! "

" Don't! "

" By birth they may be County," Mrs. Pontypool murmured. " But by manners——"

" Indeed, by manners——"

" By manners! . . ."

" Crazy creatures," Mrs. Wookie crooned, " crazy-crazies! "

Mrs. Barrow agreed.

" That a certain Signor Calixfontus," she said, " followed St. Augustine over here and married a savage—and ran through his life before most people would have cared to be seen about at all, is no excuse for his descendants to behave like perfect idiots."

132

" Or to drape themselves in those loose misfits."

" Lampshades! "

" It's Vienna! "

" Teheran!! "

" Vienna or Teheran," Mrs. Pontypool said, " or the Edgware Road, *I've* never seen such a riddle! "

But Lady Anne was looking bewildered. " When Saul was troubled," she said, " David played to him. Didn't he? "

Miss Valley nodded.

" There's a Rembrandt," she said, " about it at the Hague. I remember it so well. Chiefly because of David, who is tucked away in a remote corner of the canvas, almost as if he were the signature."

" And has he got a golden September-skin like Hendrickje Stoffels? " Aurelia asked.

" Yes; and a smile like sad music."

" Oh, but I know it! "

" Well, won't somebody go to the piano? "

" Miss Wookie will," her mother said. " Won't you, Kate? And, perhaps, sing some little song besides. She knows such shoals. What was that one, my dear, that despairing, dismal one about the heliotrope? *When Heliotropes Turn Black.* It's the true story of a sailor. Or he might have been a coastguard. And he goes away. And he comes back. And, of course, he finds her dead."

" A fugue and a breath of air," Lady Anne said, " should be quite enough. Come into the drawing-room and the Miss Chalfonts can have some supper there while we play cards. A little fruit, a little wine. . . . Poor Miss Blanche is simply sinking."

Miss Wardle disappeared altogether into her *point d'espagne.*

" O heavens! " she said.

Lady Anne's drawing-room, that had belonged, upon a time, to Mrs. Henedge, who had " rescued " it from Mrs. Goodfellow, who had come by it from Mrs. Archer, who had whipped it from Lady Lawrence, who had seized it from Mrs. Jones, of whose various "improvements" (even to distant pretty little Saxon Ethel) it bore some faint chronological trace, was picking up, as well as might be expected, to be a trifle Lady Anne's. Although there were moments even still in the grey glint of morning when the room had the agitated, stricken appearance of a person who had changed his creed a thousand times, sighed, stretched himself, turned a complete somersault, sat up, smiled, lay down, turned up his toes and died of doubts. But this aspect was reserved exclusively for the housemaids and the translucent threads of dawn.

It appeared quite otherwise now.

Upon an oval table that gleamed beneath a substantial chandelier a solitary specimen of Lady Anne's fabled Dresden was set out, equivalent, in intention, to an Oriental's iris, or blossoming branch of plum.

It was her most cherished *Rape*.

With as many variations of the theme in her cabinets as the keys in which a virtuoso will fiddle a gipsy dance, it revealed the asceticism of her mind in refraining from exhibiting them all. So situated, it is certain Mrs. Henedge would have exposed the lot.

Eyes beseeching, arms imploring, fingers straining, raiment blowing, an abduction, of necessity, must be as orthodox as a wedding with a Bishop to babble it off.

Mrs. Wookie wished.

" That's precisely my fear for Kate," she said, " when she runs out to take a motor number. Somebody, some impulsive foreigner, perhaps, visiting the Cathedral, might stop the car and capture her, and carry her away, possibly as far as Ringsea-Ashes, before she could resist. And there, I should hope, Mr. Walsh would marry them before they went on."

" She'll have many a million, I dare say, before that occurs," Miss Wardle observed. " People aren't handcuffed, seized, gagged and pinioned. Are they? "

" Still, foreigners visit the Cathedral—even blacks. While I was watering my garden to-night I saw a Moor looking at me through the fence."

Mrs. Pontypool sighed.

" Ashringford's getting *too* discovered," she said. " It's becoming spoilt. Mrs. Fulleylove was telling me at the Dean's that Lolla's to finish abroad. ' And what will she gain by it? ' I said. She could pick up quite enough languages from the tourists in the Close."

" All that would be good for her."

Miss Chimney looked fiendish. "I detest all foreigners," she said.

But, from a withdrawing-room, Miss Wookie was being borne rapidly away upon the wings of a perfectly hysterical song.

" Can nobody stop her? " Mrs. Barrow asked. The human voice, in music, she considered far too explanatory. And what did it matter *what* the heliotropes did, so long as they were suppressed.

" Her *coloratura*," Mrs. Wookie observed, " most surely improves. Although, to vibrate like Fräulein Schuster isn't done in a day."

Notwithstanding, upon the verandah, Miss Valley and Aurelia were sketching out a valse. Gently, with gowns grasped, through the moonlit spaces they twirled, the Historian gazing up abstractedly at the Cathedral towers.

" I lay you ten to one she gets it! " she cried.

" Of course, if she persists she'll prevail."

" I wish she were dead."

" Surely the world is large enough for us all."

" But I need a *Life*."

Aurelia glanced about her timidly. The solemnity of their shadows startled her.

" Though, indeed, when my investigations are over in these parts, I hope never to set foot in Ashringford again. Never, Never, Never, Never, Never, Never! "

" Some of the Spanish saints were so splendid, weren't they? "

" Oh, Aurelia—not another."

" But try a man this time."

" Man, or woman! " Miss Valley said.

" Or edit letters. Those of King Bomba to the Queen of Snowland require revision badly."

" And drown the text in the notes! "

" Make an anthology."

" *Euh*, that's so messy! "

Aurelia reversed. " Mrs. Shamefoot won't die," she said, " unless we kill her."

" Luckily, there's the climate. The air here has been called a moist caress."

" It's a poor prospect anyway."

" How I wish she were dead! "

" She's like some heavy incense, don't you think? "

Miss Valley became visionary.

" At the back of her mind," she said, " in some strange way, she's convinced her spirit will be caught in colour, and remain merged in it, as long as the glass endures."

" Has she said so? "

" Certainly not. But in our profession naturally one knows. . . . And my intuition tells me that if an atom of her, a teeny-weeny particle, *isn't* woven into the window, she'll be very cruelly chagrined."

Aurelia blinked, uncertain.

" And when would one know? " she inquired.

" Not, of course, until after she were dead."

" I call it really rather disgraceful."

" Why . . .? "

" Because, by the time she'll have done, St. Dorothy will be too disturbed to be nice. Nobody would go into it unless they were obliged. All the tranquillity would be gone. I'd never enjoy a quiet minute there again."

" My dear, that's selfish. Besides, you're scarcely two months in the year here ever, are you? "

" I should still think it horrid."

" Nonsense. Beyond a little vanity, it's hard to explain exactly what the idea indicates. But I'm sure it points to something."

" Earthiness. The extremes of it. Earth spirit! "

" Oh, more. And even if it did *not*, Mrs. Shamefoot can furnish an opera-box as very few others can. And if one can furnish an opera-box one should be able to fill in a window."

" I can imagine her asleep in a rather boring Louis the Sixteenth bedroom with a window on Sloane Square."

" Why not in Sloane Street? Over the shop. Though if you troubled to get a directory, you'd see she doesn't live that end of town at all."

But Miss Pontypool was singing now.

" Paris! Paris! Paris! Paris! O Paris! Cité de joie! Cité d'amour. . . .'"

" It's the arietta of *Louise.*"

" I knew it couldn't be David."

Like a riband flung in carnival the voice trailed away across the night.

" Poor girl! If her lines are cast in Ashringford. . . . For an instant she brought almost into this ghastly garden the glamour of the Rue de la Paix."

" Is it policy? The Miss Chalfonts will be on the floor."

" What does it matter, if they are? "

But, peeping through the window, Aurelia was unprepared to find the Miss Chalfonts listening intently while the tears were streaming from their eyes.

XV

THE municipal museum in Ghost Street was rarely, if ever, thronged, especially after noon.

" You can have the key," the wife of the custodian said, " if you want it. But there's nothing whatever inside."

And the assertion, sometimes, would spare her husband the weariness of struggling into a pair of black and silver trousers and vague historic tunic that was practically a tea. For in Ashringford, the Corporation, like a diver in a tank, was continually plunging back into the past.

" Since it pleases visitors to catch a last glimpse of this vanishing England," the Mayor had said, " *and if Stratford can*; why . . .! "

And after the customary skirmishing of the Board, and reconciliatory garden-party, a theatrical tailor had been beckoned to, from Covent Garden, who had measured half the town.

And now, beneath the grey horse-chestnut trees, where stood " the Fountain," round which, of a summer morning, the " native " women clustered, chatting charmingly, as they sold each other flowers, or posing, whenever they should be invited, to anxious artists for a shilling an hour, an enchanted American, leaning, observant, from a window of the Cresswell Arms, might almost fancy that, what with the determined duennas thronging to the Cathedral, and darting chambermaids holding long obtrusive envelopes, and tripping shepherdesses and dainty goose-girls, and occasionally, even, some pale, ring-eyed-powdered-nervous Margaret, with empty pitcher and white-stockinged feet, it was still the threshold of the thirteenth century.

"There's nothing in the museum, whatever," the woman repeated. "Nothing at all." And she added almost desperately: "It's where they keep the rubbish."

But Mrs. Shamefoot was not accustomed to be baulked.

"There're the sepulchral urns, and the tear-bottles, at any rate," she said, "and there's a good skeleton, I believe?"

"Yes, marm. There is that."

"Well, then . . ." And pushing apart the light gilt gates, she swept inside. And even if it were only for the fascinating fanlight on the stairs, she was glad that she had come.

And there was also a mirror! The unexpected shock of the thing brought a flush of pleasure to her cheek. She had hardly hoped to find so much.

"Marvellous woman," she exclaimed, going up to it, with an amicable nod, "where've you been?"

She was looking bewitching beyond measure, she believed, bound in black ribands, with a knot like a pure white butterfly under her chin.

And, to her astonishment, there were mirrors, or their equivalents, upon most of the walls.

"That habit of putting glass over an oil painting," she murmured, "makes always such a good reflection, particularly when the picture's *dark*. Many's the time I've run into the National Gallery on my way to the Savoy and tidied myself before the Virgin of the Rocks. . . ."

And selecting a somewhat spindle-legged settee she glanced yearningly around.

It was the room of the Blueharnis Bequest.

In a place of prominence, unmistakable, was the Dehell portrait of the donor, leaning against a door, in full uniform, the arms folded, the eyes fixed, dangling a sword.

What could have happened?

Anxiously, for a clue, she scanned the pendant of his wife, a billowy, balloon-like creature, leading by a chain of frail convolvulus a prancing war-horse. But the mystery still remained.

Near by, upon a screen (being stored for her), was the *Miss Millicent Mutton* of Maclise. Here, in a party pinafore, *Mrs. Henedge* was seen riding recklessly upon a goat clasping a pannier of peaches and roses while smiling down at an angelic little boy who, with a thistle and a tambourine, was urging the nanny on.

Eventually, authorities affirmed, the canvas would find its way to the South Kensington Museum, where (besides being near to dear Father . . . and to old Father . . . and the Oratory) there was a room ready waiting to receive it where it would be perfectly happy and at home.

And as one work will beget another, Mrs. Pontypool, not to be outdone, had contributed an ancestral portrait of a lady, reclining upon a canopy, plainly prostrate, beneath the hot furnaces, and the fiery skies, of Manchester. . . .

But, for the most part, as was but fitting for a Cathedral town, the mildly Satanic school of Heironymus Bosch was chiefly to the fore.

Yet, whimsically wistful, an elderly frame in curtains was waiting to be found. Leisurely, Mrs. Shamefoot rose.

That something singularly wicked was concealed beneath the hangings she had no doubt.

And indeed it was " *Le thé à l'Anglaise*, chez Lucrezia Borgia," in which an elegant and radiant Lucrezia, tea-pot in hand, was seen admiring the indisposition of her guests like a naughty child.

A glass of flowers by Fantin brought her to herself.

"If I could feel it were all arranged!" she murmured. "Unless this window-quibbling ceases, I'll soon be in my grave. And Soco, I'm confident, could not be counted upon, even for the simplest cross. He'd marry again. The brute!"

She looked out across a half-wild garden to the Asz. Beyond the broad bridges, the peaked hayricks, sprinkling the hills, stood sharp, like pyramids, against the sky. There was something monstrous and disquieting in their shapes that thrilled her. To be an Independent upon some promontory, she mused, above the sea; a landmark; perhaps a shrine! . . .

White birds, like drifting pearls, would weave their way about her, examining her with their desolate empty eyes.

Or to be a lighthouse; looped in lights!

Although to search out some poor face when it the least expected it would be carrying ill-nature, perhaps, to a rather far extreme. Better some idle tower. But in England towers so seldom mellowed rightly. They were too rain-washed, weather-beaten, wind-kissed, rugged; they turned tragic and outlived themselves; they became such hags of things; they grew dowdy and wore snapdragons; objects for picnics; rendezvous of lovers, haunts of vice . . .; they were made a convenience of by owls; they were scarred by names; choked by refuse, and in the end they got ghoulish and took to too much ivy, and came toppling down.

She stood oppressed.

Over the darkly gleaming water of the Asz a boat passed by with cordings like the strings of some melancholy instrument. From the deserted garden below an odour of burning leaves loitered up to her. The long pink Infidels flared stiffly from the shade.

"Heigh-ho," she yawned, "one can't play fast and loose for ever. . . ." And she turned away, dolefully, through the damp deserted rooms.

A piece of tessellated pavement, a sandled foot, detained her. "Street!" she murmured, stooping down, enthralled.

The frou-frou of the custodian's skirts disturbed her.

"Such a mixture of everything as there is; a country Cluny!"

"I dare say, marm. I've never been round the worruld; I've lived in Ashringford, man and boy, these sixty years."

"Indeed; that's why you look so young!"

"I beg your pardon, marm?"

"I say, that's why you look so *young!*"

And startled by his historic attire, she trailed slowly towards the door, gazing back at him across her shoulder, with one arm stretched before, the other lingering behind, in the attitude of a nymph evading a satyr upon a Kylix.

It was a relief to hear voices! Chatting beneath an immaterial study of the sunset breeze, she beheld the ample form of Sumph.

"And in Act IV," she was saying, "the husband *pretends* to go away. But, of course, he doesn't! He goes only a little distance. . . . And the ' curtain ' should be beautiful! Lovely it ought to be. The birds all singing as if their last hour had come. And Miss Compostella and Mr. Chalmers——"

"Is your mistress anywhere about?" Mrs. Shamefoot interrupted her.

Sumph smiled.

"Why, no," she said, "she's not. I'm here with Mrs. Henedge's maid, just taking a look round."

"Really? . . ."

"Whenever I'm able I like to encourage anything that's Art."

"And how do you like Ashringford?"

"I like it. It puts me in mind of the town Dick Whittington came to when all the bells were ringing."

142

"You've been up the tower! "

" It didn't seem worth while. They told us before-hand we could never see *back there*. . . . But we watched them pull the bells. Quite a receipt of their own they seemed to have. Such swingings and pausings and noddings and rushings. You should have seen the dowdies run! And in such bonnets. As Thérèse remarked, it was an education in botany."

" Oh-h-h! "

There came a cry.

Mrs. Henedge's maid was before the Borgia *thé*.

Nodding sympathetically to Sumph, Mrs. Shame-foot disappeared.

XVI

" EVER since the accident," Lady Georgia said, " she has been going about in such heavens of joy. I've seldom seen anyone so happy."

Mrs. Guy Fox passed a hand across her eyes.

" It fell," she remarked, " so suddenly; I was in my bath."

Miss Compostella helped herself to honey.

" I fear St. Dorothy's badly damaged."

" Half of it is down."

" Oh no, dear; not half."

" It's as if the gods granted it to her," Lady Georgia declared; " she's been so brave."

" Such gusts of wind! The way they pulled the bushes——"

" How did it happen, exactly? "

" A pair of scissors, it appears, was left upon the scaffolding, and caught the lightning's eye."

" What a dreadful thing! "

Mrs. Fox shuddered.

" That the Cathedral should submit to be struck," she said, " strikes me as being so strange. It never has before."

" Lady Anne has twice 'phoned."

" . . . Surely not already? "

" Before breakfast, too! "

" Polite. . . ."

Lady Georgia rolled her eyes.

" What is one to do with a person," she demanded, " who cannot feel the spell of a beautiful supreme thing like Tintoretto's *Crucifixion* ? "

" And where is she now? "

" Oh, my dear, she's wandering exultant about the house. She's been doing it since six."

" Leave her," Mr. Guy Fox advised. " Perhaps presently she'll come down and have a good cry."

" Darling Biddy, she's been divinely patient. But the strain was becoming too much for her. It was undermining her health."

" Holding ten cathedrals at arm's-length must have been terribly tiring."

" I had an idea it was quite the other way. In any case, thank Heaven, the wrangling's over. Done."

" I wouldn't say that. But clearly a difficulty is removed. They're sure to secure her for the Restorations."

" My maid has asked if she may go over and see the ruins," Miss Compostella said.

" She should take the bridle-path through the fields," Lady Georgia murmured, rising to welcome Mrs. Shamefoot as she came in.

Over a rug that suggested a summer morning Mrs. Shamefoot skimmed, pale in cloud-white laces, her hands buried beneath the flimsy plumage of a muff, like some soul who (after a tirade or two) would evaporate and take flight.

" You may kiss me," she murmured wistfully, " but kiss me carefully."

" I heard you at the telephone as I crossed the hall."

" Lady Anne re-rang."

" I hope she was pleasant."

" No. She was only half-charming, if you know; she was nice, without being nicer. . . . But one feels she's climbing down. Of course, I told her, without the approbation of all Ashringford, I wouldn't for the world . . . and, on her side, she spoke of making a ragoût with the remains."

" She's so tasteless," Lady Georgia exclaimed. " But there it is, many people seem to imagine that a stained-glass window is nothing of the kind unless some over-good-looking young saint is depicted in bathing drawers and half-an-inch of water."

Mrs. Shamefoot raised her muff beneath her chin. " Soco's so silly," she said. " He'd fire at anything like that with his revolver. And, oh, Mr. Guy Fox . . . I've got to scold you. Standing beneath my window and calling me by my name millions and millions of times was fearfully indiscreet. . . ."

" I thought you'd be interested to know."

" ' It's down,' you said, ' it's down.' The servants must have wondered what you meant! Though it's really rather odd; when your voice disturbed me, I was having such a curious-funny dream. People were digging me up for reliques. . . ."

" Here's your coffee, dear."

" All I need, darling, is a Railway Guide. I must return at once to town; I'm so busy! "

" Remain until to-morrow," Miss Compostella said, " and travel back with me."

" But, Julia, you're not leaving us so soon! "

" I must. You know I'm in despair with my helmet for the Garsaint piece. I do not care about myself in it at all: it's too *stiff*. And the crown; I'm sure the crown's too timid."

But Mrs. Guy Fox was reading aloud some extracts of a letter from her son, a dutiful diplomat who, even when fast asleep, it was said, suggested the Court of St. James.

" Just now," she read, " the Judas trees along the banks of the Bosphorus are coming into flower. The colour of these trees is extraordinary. They are neither red nor violet, and at evening they turn a sort of agony of rose."

" Delicious! " Lady Georgia said, staring at Atalanta in dismay. There were moments, especially in the early morning, when she alarmed her mother. Moments when she looked remotely Japanese. . . .

" No; there's nothing in the paper at all, except that the Wirewells have arrived," Lady Castleyard said, stepping out upon the lawn.

Mrs. Shamefoot joined her.

After the gale a yellow branch lay loose beneath each tree, making the park appear to be carpeted by some quite formal silk. The morning was fine with courageous crazy clouds.

" You're tired? "

" A little," Lady Castleyard confessed. " All this death makes me melancholy."

" I expect it's merely Lionel! "

" Lionel? But I'm not tired of Lionel. Only, now and then, I long rather for a new aspect. . . ."

" Do you suppose, if there were no men in the world, that women would frightfully mind? "

" I don't know, really. . . . What a pity to leave that gloriously bound book out all night! "

They turned aside through a wicket-gate into an incidental garden.

At periods, upon the enclosing walls, stood worn lead figures of cupid gardeners, in cavalier hats and high loose boots and cunning gloves, leaning languidly upon their rakes, smiling seraphically over the gay rings of flowers that broke the grass.

" Age holds no horrors for me," Mrs. Shamefoot said, " now, any more. Some day I'll have a house here and I'll grow old quite gracefully."

" Surely with age one's attractions should increase. One should be irresistible at ninety."

"A few of us, perhaps, may. You, dear Dirce, will——"

" But in Ashringford! You used always to say it would be at Versailles, or Vallombrosa, or Verona, or Venice; a palladio palace on the Grand Canal. Somewhere with a *V!* "

" I remember . . .; although I was tempted too rather, wasn't I, towards Arcachon. And that's an *A!*"

" Poor Soco. He'll be so surprised. . . ."

" It's a pity, whenever he speaks, he's so very disappointing."

" Still, there'll be the bill. . . ."

" Well, he could scarcely have seriously supposed I'd throw myself away upon a lancet! Besides, I believe I'll be desired somehow more when I'm gone. What good am I here? "

" My dear, you compose in flowers. You adorn life. You have not lived in vain."

They were in the dogs' cemetery.

Lady Castleyard tapped a little crooked cross.

" One fears," she said, " that Georgia must have poisoned them all for the sake of their epitaphs."

" Here come the children! "

" And remember, Frank," Fräulein was warning Master Fox, in her own wonderful Hanoverian way, " not to pursue Mirabel too much towards the end. It makes her hot."

They were preparing to play at Pelléas.

Lady Georgia insisted that her children should practise only purely poetic games. She desired to develop their souls and bodies harmoniously at the same time.

" Remember the chill she caught as Nora! " Fräulein said. " And, Dawna, must I re-implore you not to pick up the sun-money with your hands? Misericordia! One might think your father was a banker."

" I do so love the sun! "

" Do you, dear? "

Obviously, it was an occasion to kiss and form a group.

XVII

"CERTAINLY I should object to milk a cow," Miss Compostella said. "Why?"

Sumph smiled.

"I see so many," she said. "One, the prettiest possible thing, the very living, breathing image of the Alderney that you engaged, miss, to walk on in *The Princess of Syracuse*."

"It would be the signal," Miss Compostella said, "often for a scuffle."

"And don't I know it!" said Sumph.

"Although to me it was always extraordinary that Miss Elcock, who almost fainted whenever she encountered it in the wings, would become indifferent to the point of being tossed the instant the curtain rose. She was too preoccupied about appearing young, I suppose, to care about anything else, her own part included."

"Oh no, miss. She was a great, great actress. Watching her in certain scenes, how cold my hands would grow! The blood would fly to my heart!"

The invaluable woman grew nostalgic.

"I fear you don't delight in the country, somehow, as you should."

"I don't know, miss. Ashringford amuses me. I find myself dying with laughter here several times a day."

"Indeed——"

"Naturally not in the house. It's too much like a sanatorium for that. Every time I come to you along the corridors I feel just as if I was going to visit some poor sick soul and had forgotten my flowers."

Miss Compostella gave an arranging touch to a bouquet of blue berries above her ear.

"I hope you passed a pleasant afternoon," she said, "among the ruins."

"It was lovely. I sat on a piece of crumbled richness in the long grass for over an hour. Afterwards I took tea at the Closed House with Thérèse. She was so busy with her needle. 'I shall need a frock for my conversion,' Mrs. Henedge told her the other day, 'and another for my reconversion, in case that's necessary.' 'But fashions change so quickly, madame,' Thérèse said to her. 'And so do I,' she said; 'I can travel a long way in a week.' Chopping and changing! But it's to be quite a decided little frock for all that. Very plain. With some nice French buttons. The *other* is one of those curious colour contrasts. . . . So sickly. But rather smart. A discord of lemon, pink, and orange. And I came back, miss, to Stockingham, by way of the Asz, in spite of Signora Spaghetti. 'Never walk by the water-side,' she said to me, when I was a child. That's why we left Stratford. Because of the Avon."

"But surely the Thames——"

"Bless you, no !"

"And you saw nothing of the Bishop?"

"His pinched white face frightened me. It gave me such a turn. . . .

Weep, willow, weep,
Willow, willow, weep,
For the cross that's mine is difficult to bear."

Miss Compostella interposed.

"You needn't pack up everything," she remarked.

"It's my impatience! I could sing when I think we're returning home to-morrow. If it's only to escape the housekeeper here. For we had quite a quarrel just now. . . . 'Where's your wedding ring?' she says. 'I never wear it,' I replied. 'It makes one's hand look so bourgeoise. And don't you go flinging your nasty aspersions over me,' I said, ' for I won't have it.' "

" Quite right."

" My word. I was very carefully brought up. My mother was most tyrannical, especially with us girls. Why I wasn't even allowed to read *The Vicar of Wakefield* until after I was married. . . . Not that I didn't belong to a Rabelais—lovers—Society by the time I was twelve."

" What, in Stratford? " Miss Compostella wondered, taking up with lassitude the manuscript of a play left with her by Mrs. Shamefoot (before the accident), in the expectation of obtaining an interest at the Palace by overwhelming Miss Hospice by an eternal and delicate debt of thanks.

It was a *Tristram and Isolde.*

" *Brangane and Isolde,*" she read. " *Deck chairs. Isolde making lace. Soft music.*

Br. But what makes you think he's so fond of you, my dear?

Is. He presses my hand so beautifully.

Br. You know he does that to *everybody.*

Is. O-h?

Br. Take my advice. *I* should never marry him.

Is. Really? Why not?

Br. He would leave you.

Is. Nonsense!

Br. He has ears like wings. . . .

Is. Is that all?

" Not such a bad beginning," Miss Compostella commented. " But why must Isolde be so impatient to confide to the waves her age? ' I'm exactly nine-and-twenty.' I cannot see that it helps. And why, oh, why," she murmured, rising to her feet, " when Tristram inquires for her, should Brangane lose her head so, and say 'She's out, she's not at home, she isn't there'? Were she to reply quite calmly, almost like a butler, 'The family's away,' or, 'I expect them home in about a fortnight,' it should be amply sufficient."

A lazy ripple of strings surprised her.

" What is that——? "

" I don't know, miss, I'm sure. It sounds like *Pippa Passes*."

" Well, go and see."

" It brings back to me the reading Mrs. Steeple gave at the Caxton Hall when I, Miss Falconhall and her fiancé received Press tickets. . . . Coming away, foolish fellow, he slipped on a piece of cabbage-stalk and snapped his coledge bone."

" Can you make out who is serenading us? "

" It's the Honourable Mrs. Shamefoot," Sumph informed. Pacing beneath a magnificence of autumnal trees, Mrs. Shamefoot was strolling slowly up and down with a guitar.

" She's been on stilts all day," Sumph said.

Miss Compostella coiled an arm across her head.

" Give me a phenacetin powder," she exclaimed, " at once. For what with the crash the Cathedral made in falling, and your silly jabber, and her guitar . . .!"

XVIII

"THE little turquoise flower you admired, my beloved, on Wednesday, is known as *Fragment of Happiness*. You will find it again in some of *Dürer's* drawings. Oh, George! . . . On my desk there is an orange-tree. How it makes me yearn, dear, for the South! I count my oranges. Eight poor, pale, crabbed oranges. Like slum cripples. I think of Seville now. Yes. To-morrow. Absolutely. But, dearest, *downstairs*, Rosalba Roggers sometimes sallies up. She saw us together last time and begged so to be told who my wonderful big child was with the tragic face. Five o'clock, dear. And don't be late as you usually are.   M.

"*P.S.*—I will carry some of your troubles, if you will send them to me with your thoughts.

"*P.P.S.*—You say I blush! When, I wonder, shall I learn to have a mask of my own?"

"Minx!" Mrs. Calvally exclaimed. "The snake. . . ."
She seemed stupefied, stunned.
"I merely opened his paint-box," she began, stammering to herself.
"Mamma! . . ."
And, as if to demonstrate that domestic drama is not entirely tired of its rather limited tricks, her little son Raphael entered the room at that minute and rushed right into her arms.
He came. . . .
She stooped. . . .
"My dear!"
And now she was calm again, complacent, with all her old tranquillity of gardens.

" Oh, how ugly! . . ."

" Where, my precious? "

" And is it a present, too? "

For the artist's anniversary Miss Thumbler had despatched a door-knocker, wrought in bronze, that represented a woebegone, wan Amour.

" By all means," Mrs. Calvally had said, " let us put it up. I will call a carpenter. And some of the mirrors, as well, need glueing. . . ."

And the gift decidedly had eclipsed her own humble offering of the Hundred Best Pictures, in photogravure, that did not appear to have aroused in him all the interest that they might.

" Mrs. Asp and Mrs. Thumbler are in the drawing-room."

" Are they, my pet? "

" And Mrs. Asp is concealing such a lovely-looking thing. All wrapped up. It must be something for papa."

" Come along and let us see."

" Don't sigh, mamma. It bores me to hear you sigh."

" I'm so sorry George isn't in," Mrs. Calvally said, as she lounged leisurely round the huge Ming screen that began her drawing-room. " But he went out, quite early, almost before it was light, to make a Canaletto of the space before White Hall."

" I believe he's unusually busy. . . . So I hear! " Mrs. Asp announced.

" No. Not so very. . . . He's making Mrs. Jeffreys at present in all her jewels? or, at any rate, more than he usually likes. And the old Duke of Spitalfields. And the cartoons of a country church. . . ."

Mrs. Thumbler began to purr.

" And he obliges Mira," she said, " nearly every day. And in such varieties of poses! Even as Absalom, swinging from a tree."

" I know. He raves about her. He told me he looked

upon her almost as an inspiration," Mrs. Calvally replied, confident that the "almost" would be repeated to haunt Miss Thumbler for days.

"All the same, quite between ourselves, I confess, I wish he didn't. It's making her so vain! Lately (I'm ashamed to tell you) she's taken to wear *a patch*. A crescent-moon-shaped affair above the lip that gives her such an o-ri-gi-nal expression. Really, sometimes in the street . . . Well, I won't go out with her again. I let her take the dog."

Mrs. Asp untied an ermine stole.

"My dear," she exclaimed, "do be careful. When it comes to dragging a dumb animal about as a chaperon one gets generally misunderstood."

"But what am I to do? Mira's so sensitive. I dare hardly say a word. Although those pen-and-ink embroideries Mr. Calvally made for her, charming as they are, are only fit for the house."

"I wasn't aware he had ever made her any," Mrs. Calvally said. "I'm sure he never made pen-and-ink embroideries for me!"

"Occupation," Mrs. Asp reflected airily, "is an admirable thing, especially for a man. It restricts restlessness as a rule."

"How you comfort me! He talks of a farm-house now near Rome."

Mrs. Thumbler shuddered.

"I should hate to keep an Italian cow," she said. "I should be afraid of it!"

"But *we* should be Byzantine. Just peacocks, stags and sheep. . . ."

"The danger of Italy," Mrs. Asp observed, "is, it tends to make one florid. One expands there so. . . . Personally, I go all to poppy-seed directly. I cannot keep pace with my ideas. And then I fall ill, and have to have a nurse. Shall I ever forget the creature I had last year! My dear Mrs. Calvally, she looked just about as stable as the young woman on the cover of a valse. Unfortunately, I was too exhausted to object. But I simply couldn't endure her. She made me so uneasy. A habit of staring vaguely into space whenever she spoke to me would make me shiver; I began to believe she must be in league with the doctor; that she was hiding something, keeping something back. . . . At last, one day I collected all my strength together and sat up in my bed and pointed towards the door. After that, I took a nun, who was quite rapacious for martyrdom. But all that was ever allowed to her was, sometimes, to get cold feet."

" And what are you doing now? "

Mrs. Asp relaxed.

" At present," she said, " I'm preparing a *Women Queens of England.*"

" Isn't it idle—to insist? "

" Not as euphony. *The Queens* of England, somehow, sound so bleak. And, really, rather a brigade. . . . More like history! "

At the portentous word Master Raphael rolled down upon the floor.

Mrs. Asp considered him. She was old-fashioned enough to believe it necessary for a young thing, when it gaped, to know exactly where to place its hand.

" Does he take after his papa? " she asked.

" I hardly know. He loves to flick his tongue up and down the rough paint of a picture, and to cool his cheek along the shrubberies on my fans."

" He promises! " Mrs. Asp declared.

" But so wicked. Yesterday Princess Schara came to show George a fan. You know her husband used to paint the most wonderful fans. Poor man, in the end he became so decorative that he died! His last fan—would you care to see it?—is such a muddle that very few people can discover what it means. And now Raphael has made it utterly impossible."

"Most modern fans are so ill and sickly," Mrs. Thumbler observed, " I hope nothing will happen to your courageous little boy."

Mrs. Calvally lit—one of those . . .

It was a caprice of hers that could still charm, thrill and fascinate a wayward husband.

He had studied her too, thus, at three different angles on a single canvas. More vagabond, possibly, than the Charles, or the Richelieu, or the Lady Alice Gordon of Reynolds, but, nevertheless, with not one whit less style.

" How stately the studio is," Mrs. Asp said, a little confused. " A perfect paradise! "

" I regret I've nothing to show you much that's new. You've seen his joy-child for the top of a fountain, I expect, before? "

But Mrs. Thumbler did not seem cast down.

" I admire your plain black curtains," she said, " and, oh, where did you get these? "

Continually, Mrs. Calvally would design an eccentric frame for her husband's pictures. It was a pathetic attempt, perhaps, on her side, to identify herself in his career.

For, indeed, she was notoriously indifferent to art.

She was one of those destined to get mixed over Monet and Manet all their life.

The exhibition of some " lost " masterpiece, in Bond Street, was what she most enjoyed, when, if not too crowded, she could recline upon a sofa and turn out the lining to her purse.

" I'm such a wretched, wicked housekeeper," she would say. " And were it not for an occasional missing Gainsborough, George, I should never know what I had."

" Bristling with intellect," Mrs. Asp pronounced, laying down the fan, " and I seem to catch a face in it, too. Little Mrs. Steeple's! . . ."

" Oh, quite——"

" Poor thing! She says Sir Samuel has become so vigorous lately. It nearly kills her every evening waiting for his slap."

" We were at Smith Square on Sunday," Mrs. Calvally said, " and sitting at her feet found Julia's new man—Charley Chalmers! "

" And I suppose a god? " Mrs. Asp inquired.

" Not at all. It's a doll-like, child-like, Adamy sort of face, and very healthy."

" Dear Julia, I've seen nothing of her since the Sappho supper-party Mrs. Henedge gave in the spring."

" I hear she's been safely landed now about a week."

" One can hardly credit it! "

" She sent us a jar of Ashringford honey," Mrs. Thumbler said, " recently. Perfectly packed, in half-a-field of hay."

" She takes a kind of passionate pleasure in her bees. And Mr. Brookes helps her in them, muffled up in all the newest veils."

" He's been away now so long. He might be almost learning to be a priest," Mrs. Asp remarked, as Lady Listless came in.

" I heard a thrush singing in the park," she said. " It was so attractive. I don't know what came over me! Are my eyes wet still with tears? I held back one to bring your husband (I saw the many-happy-returns in *The World*), but I lost it. It rolled, unluckily, under the wheels of a miserable motor bus. But I managed to get another! So I carried myself as if I were Lily, Lady Ismore, and got nearly safe with it, when it fell down as the lift stopped."

" You should have warned the boy! "

" I did. . . ."

" The incredible thrush! " Mrs. Asp exclaimed.

" Very likely it wasn't totally the thrush. I won't

be positive. It may have been merely the reaction after Mr. Hurreycomer's Private View. His *Susanna!* ... Have you seen it? ... A young woman (my dear, his wife) splashing herself in some perfectly lilac water. ... And the Elders. ... Oh, they are all portraits. ..."

" Tell me about the Elders," Mrs. Calvally begged.

" Your husband. *Most* prominent."

" But George isn't forty! "

" Are you sure? "

" It's incredible, in any case, that an insignificant stupid thing like Carla could interest even Elders," Mrs. Asp remarked, getting up. " Moreover," she continued, drawing on a glove, " she revels in making herself needlessly hideous; it appeals to her sense of truth. Added to which," she rambled on, " his candid studies of women are simply hateful. ..."

" Brutal! " Mrs. Thumbler opined.

" Has anybody seen my stole? "

" And, remember, Rose," Mrs. Calvally said, returning it to her, " for Friday, it's *you* who've got the tickets! "

" I shan't forget. But since it's likely to be a debate, don't expect to see me smart. I shall simply wear my old, soiled, peach-charmeuse. ..."

" My dear, don't bother to dress! "

Mrs. Asp hesitated.

" I trust that nobody of yours," she said, " is ill or stricken, for there's a strange old man seated on the stairs, with such a terrific bag of tools! "

Mrs. Calvally chuckled.

" I conclude it's only the carpenter," she explained, " who has come to pass a screw through Miss Mira's charming consumptive Amour! "

XIX

"Don't the hills look soaked through and through with water?"

"My dear, I don't know!"

"If you don't object, I'll go back, I think, to bed."

"What can you expect at the fall of the leaf?"

"But, except for the evergreens, all the leaves are down."

"Well, last winter, it rained so, and it rained so, that the drawing-room became a lake. All my beautiful blue silk chairs . . .; and a few gold fish I'm attached to were floated right out of their bowl, and swam upstairs into Thérèse's room."

"Ashringford's becoming dreadfully disagreeable."

"Patience. The sun will come up presently. Even now it's doing something behind the Cathedral. It usually takes its time to pick a path across St. Dorothea."

Now that she had actually abandoned it, St. Dorothy, for Mrs. Henedge, had become St. Dorothea.

"Hannah was telling us the night it fell she noticed devils sort-of-hobble-stepping beneath the trees."

"My dear, she tells such lies. One never can believe her. Only the other day she broke the child's halo off my plaster Anthony and then declared she didn't."

"The most wonderful name in all the world for any child," Winsome said, "is Diana. Don't you agree? Your gardener intended to call his daughter Winifred, but I was just in time!"

"There now, there's a pretty motive for a walk. Save Mrs. Drax's baby. It's to be christened Sobriety, to-day, at half-past-two. Such a shame!"

" But I should miss Goosey."

" Winsome, lately, had taken quite a fancy to Goosey, while risking their necks together upon the scaffolding of St. John's."

" You see so much of him. The Miss Chalfonts, in comparison, aren't to be compared."

" Don't ever speak of them! "

" Why not? "

" I've such a shock in store."

" Yes; what is it? "

" The Miss Chalfonts have scratched."

" Scratched! . . ."

" Their Guardi."

" What does it matter if they have? I've really no need for any *more* pictures. People seem to think that St. John's is going to be a Gallery, or something of the kind."

" And I've something else to tell you."

" Sit down and tell me here."

" While we were leaning from the campanile an idea occurred to me. Another opera."

" Bravo! You shall kiss my hand."

" I start *fortissimo!* The effect of the Overture will be the steam whistle that summons the factory hands. *Such a hoot!* . . ."

" But you'll finish what you're doing? "

Since his arrival in Ashringford he had been at work on a *Gilles de Raie,* an act of which already was complete. The sextet between Gilles and his youthful victims bid fair, Mrs. Henedge declared, to become the most moving thing in all opera. While the lofty theme for Anne de Bretagne and the piteous *Prière* of the little Marcelle seemed destined, also, to be popular.

" I'm so glad, for, naturally, while the building's in progress I have to be on the spot. And I do so hate to be alone. . . . I cannot bear it. I like to have you with me! "

" Still, you've got Monsignor Parr. . . ."

" Dear, charming, delightful Monsignor Parr! "

" Are there any more new designs? "

" No. But Mr. Calvally is constructing some confessionals for us utterly unlike the usual *cabines-de-bains*. . . . And apropos of them, I've something serious to say to you. I'm sorry to have to say it . . . for I'd really much rather not! "

" I'm listening."

" It's about *Andrew*. Those Dégas danseuses he sends to you . . . on letter cards. . . . I know, I know, *I know!* And, perhaps, if he didn't scribble over them . . . But—how very often have I said it?—I never liked him. That violet muffler. And the no-collar. . . ."

" Why, what? "

" Here is a card that came for you. When I saw it I assure you it made me feel quite quaint and queer. *I thought it was for me!* "

" Oh, but you couldn't! "

" 'My dear old Sin, do ask me not to write to you again. Or answer my letters properly.' "

" I wish Andrew wouldn't correspond with you in that coarse way. Ever! At least not while you're at the Closed House. What must the postman think? "

" That's nerves! You mustn't begin to worry like Lady Brassknocker. Her apprehension of the servants is a disease."

" But a postman isn't a simple servant. One doesn't dismiss him. I like my letters. Here is one from Atossa Listless. She says Lady Castleyard and Mrs. Shamefoot are going to Cannes. And there's another difficulty apparently: whether the window shall open, or *not*."

" How capricious the Palace is."

" Mrs. Shamefoot is ill with strain. Lady Listless says she speaks of nothing now but death. She says it's almost shocking to hear her. Nothing else amuses her at all. . . . And it gets so gloomy and so monotonous."

" Probably the casino——"

" That's what they try to hope. At present she's continually cabling to India about her pall. After the coffin she says she'll have violins—four: Kubelik, Zimbaliśt, Kreisler, and Melsa. . . . And no doubt Dina will send a splendid sheaf of something from the shop."

Winsome tossed back his hair and half clouded his eyes. He glazed them.

" Wait! " he murmured, moving to the piano.

Mrs. Henedge obeyed, expeċtant, upright, upon the tip of her chair. She knew the signs. . . . Her finger-tips hovering at her heart caged an Enchantress Satin Rose.

> " Lillilly-là, lillilly-là,
> Là, là, là.
> Lillilly, lillilly, lillilly-là,
> Lillilly-là, lillilly-là,
> Lillilly, lillilly, lillilly-là,
> L-à-à-à. . . ."

" Well; really! . . ."

" I couldn't help it. It juśt broke from me. It's *The Song of the Embalmers.* . . ."

" . . . I call it lovely! Poor Mrs. Shamefoot. That lillilly, lillilly, lillilly. One feels they really are doing something to the corpse. It's sitting up! And the long final l-à-à-à. It's dreadful. Don't they fling it down? " And with finger rigid she pointed towards the floor.

" It's good of you to like it," Winsome said, with some emotion. " And here's Goosey? "

" Never lend your name, or your money, or your books, or your umbrella, or anything, to anybody— if you're wise," Goosey Pontypool remarked over his shoulder to Winsome as he pressed Mrs. Henedge's hand.

" But it isn't raining? "

" It doesn't matter. Here, they pour down dust upon you as you go by."

" It's a sign," Mrs. Henedge said, " that the houses are tenanted. Thérèse will sometimes say to me that that melancholy Miss Wintermoon must have gone away *at last* when suddenly up flies her window and a hand shakes a duster into the street."

" In Ashringford there's chatter enough indoors. You'd be surprised? "

" Well, I never know what goes on, except when the sow gets into the Dean's garden. And then I hear the screams."

" I hear everything."

" Which, invariably, you exaggerate! "

" It's no crime to exaggerate. It's a sign of vitality rather. Health . . ."

" Whisper what you've heard."

" That Mr. Pet is to marry Miss Wardle and Mr. Barrow's to be made a peer."

" Upon what grounds? "

" For doctoring the Asz. You know it used always to ooze away; he's just discovered where. While she was watering her rhododendrons he noticed. . . . Anyway, he's going to Egypt officially soon to do something to the Nile."

" How delightful for her! "

" She's advertising for a cottage at Bubastis, a bungalow, a villa. . . ."

Mrs. Henedge became staid.

" I suppose she'll get like Salabaccha now," she said. " Ah well! "

" Even so, it's much more wonderful for Jane. . . ."

" I'm at a loss to conceive anyone . . ."

" I don't know. Miss Wardle isn't, perhaps, what

164

you'd expect. When I called at Wormwood she said:
'I was so sure we should find plenty in common. *I could
feel it through the window*. I've often watched you pass.'"

"Those complicated curls of hers remind me of
the codicils to my poor dear Leslie's will."

"Who arranged the match?"

"St. Dorothy. She was expatiating on her escape
. . . 'I heard a noise,' she said, 'a sound. But country
servants are so rough. Aren't they? Breaking, dropping,
chipping things. . . . I haven't a dish that isn't
cracked. . . . So, if I didn't hurry immediately to
look out, it was because . . . because . . . because . . .
because . . . Because I was in the middle of my prayers.'

"'Had it fallen a *leetle* more your way,' he said,
'there would have been an end of them.'

"'Oh, Mr. Pet,' she said, 'What difference could
that have made to you?'"

"So simple!"

"Well, if it's true, it's the best thing possible. Now,
perhaps, we shall get rid of them *both*."

"I believe it's not at all unlikely. Wormwood's to
be let; not noisily. But, at the land agent's, nobody
could mistake the exaggerated description of the con-
servatories and the kiosk by the lake."

"Mrs. Shamefoot's searching for a house here-
abouts, isn't she?"

"Oh, Wormwood's hardly what she wants. It isn't
rustic enough. It doesn't thrill."

"Besides, she's already made an offer for the Old
Flagellites Club."

"It should suit her. That long flaying room would
make an exquisite drawing-room. And there's a
sheltered pretty garden at the back."

Winsome began twisting across his eyes a heavy,
heliotrope veil.

"Don't let me interrupt you," he murmured, "I'm
merely going to peep at the bees."

XX

LADY BARROW lolled languidly in her mouse-eaten library, a volume of mediæval Tortures (with plates) propped up against her knee. In fancy, her husband was well pinned down and imploring for mercy at Figure 3.

How eagerly, now, he proffered her the moon! How he decked her out with the stars! How he overdressed her!

Coldly she considered his case.

" Release you? Certainly not! Why should I? " she murmured comfortably, transferring him to the acuter pangs of 9.

And morally she could have started as her maid came in.

" Yes, what is it? "

" Sir S'torious is looking everywhere for your ladyship."

The difficulty the servants seemed to find in saying " Sir Sartorious," without a slovenly contraction, was frequently distressing.

Grigger, his man, would quite break down, while the housemaids tripped, and the chauffeur literally sneezed.

" Say that I'm busy."

Lady Barrow closed her book.

Something would have to be done.

" Had it been a peerage, was elocution compulsory, there need have been none of this fuss," she exclaimed.

And with her finger-ends pressed to her eyes she began to conjure up his latent baptismal names:

" Sartorious, Hugh, Wilful, Anne, Barrow. S,H,W,A,B. *Schwab!* " she murmured.

166

And loosening a pencil from her wrist, she put them sharply to the test.

" Sir Sartorious regrets——"

" Sir Hugh and Lady Barrow regret——"

" Sir Wilful and Lady Barrow much regret——"
Or even " deeply——"

" Sir Anne—— *San*——" She shuddered. Lady Barrow walked towards the door.

" Wilful! " she called, in what her maid later described as a light silvery voice, " I'm here! . . ."

But the silence oppressed her. " Presently," she reflected, " perhaps, will do. It'll be something to discuss during dinner. Although, indeed, after what's occurred, I hadn't intended to say very much to him to-night."

And apathetically she looked away across the cloud-shaded hills.

How well she knew the roads round Dawn! Here and there a tree would lift itself above the rest. . . .

The forlornness of it!

Up to the very house crept the churchyard yews, whose clipped wide windows never held a face.

And, somewhere, in the dark, dipping branches of a cedar, lurked the Raven. . . .

" I'm *all* romantic feelings," Lady Barrow murmured. " I always was. I always will be."

And from a lavender cardboard box she slipped a smart sombrero piled up with wings and wings and wings.

" What is the good? " she murmured, dispirited, as she tried it on. Still, in every shadow, of every room, Lady Barrow would store a hat.

" I never intend to lose sight of town clothes," was the explanation that she gave.

But to-day it was not essentially in vain. Scarcely had she poised it than she saw Lady Georgia's car coming up the drive.

167

" I'm perfectly ashamed," Lady Georgia began, " not to have been over before."

" Say nothing of it! "

" And so, thanks to Sir Sartorious, one may curtail one's domestic troubles. Like poor Mrs. Frobisher——"

" Who is Mrs. Frobisher? "

" She was our nearest neighbour with a soul."

" The Asz is in arrears. A short while ago even my cook went down. (Sartorious, if anything goes wrong . . .) And there were we! All of us upon our knees to her, flattering her, from the bank."

" And a Mrs. Luther Gay—such a shocking thing —sprang quite suddenly off her lawn——"

" And one of the Olneys, too, was driven home from the Dean's dance, drenched. And with her heavy head, and her thin neck, and her poinsettia-pink arms——"

" So long as it isn't bathing."

" And then there was Captain Hoey."

" Cards! "

" And Azeza Williams."

" Love! "

" And little Miss Chimney."

" Despair! "

" And Admiral van Boome."

" I heard—— "

" It makes one long to get away. The responsibility is beginning to tell."

" And so you're positively off? "

" Yes. We've got rid of Dawn to such a very pretty widow—a Mrs. Lily Carteret Brown. . . ."

" Who, at all, is she? "

" I couldn't be sure. But after a career of dissipation she seems delighted to settle down."

" And where *is* the great man? "

" Sartorious? He's packing."

" Packing! "

" All great men are prosaic at close quarters. Didn't you know? "

" Dear Violet——"

" Not since we were married have we been away together once."

" It should rekindle happy memories."

Lady Barrow shook the dancing, whispering things upon her hat.

" When we were first married," she said, " I was very, very wretched. I would weep, weep, weep at night! And in the morning, often, my maid would have to put my pillow-case out upon the window-ledge to dry. Fortunately, it was in Sicily, so it never took long."

" And later, what are your plans? "

" I had the project of Paris."

" Mrs. Henedge goes there too, in connection with the festas at St. John's."

" My dear, she's always covered in embroideries; one never sees her in anything else."

" She was superintending her building just now very busily as I came through the town."

" How is it getting on? "

" Fairly fast. . . . It will have a very fine front. And, of course, nothing at all behind."

" I believe it's only going to be very large——"

" Exactly! "

" When once they're gone she'll almost regret her workmen's blue sleeves."

" It must be a little lonely for her sometimes."

" I can't conceive when! She's for ever dancing round her yclept geniuses. . . . Making their death-masks, or measuring their hands. She never leaves them alone one minute."

" Of all the discoveries, Mr. Brookes appears to be the best."

" The least anxiety, perhaps——"

" That requiem he sent Biddy showed style."

" Where is she now? "

" At Cannes. Lady Ismore caught sight of her in the casino the other day, in magnificence, brilliance, beauty. . . ."

" One either admires her extremely or not at all."

" Of course, she's continually criticised."

" Sartorious thinks her colourless! "

" How?. . ."

" Pale. I don't know. He believes she makes up with chalk."

" What an idea."

" I suppose we shall receive cards for her vitrification before very long."

" Not until the spring. She wants the sun."

" She used to hate it."

" Poor Mrs. Frobisher's girl was to have taken part in the cortège."

" Cortège! "

" She's to be supported. Children singing; scattering flowers."

" What does Dr. Pantry say? "

" For the moment he objects. The *panther skins* upset him. . . ."

" Lady Anne would never hear of it! "

" On the contrary, she adores processions. They are quite her weakness."

" Depravity! "

" Biddy will be charming. I shall persuade her, if I can, to wear a crinoline."

Lady Barrow beamed.

" Take her to Madame Marathon," she said.

" I've never heard of her."

" Of course, she's rather expensive. You pay her ninety guineas for a flicker of a gown. . . ."

Lady Georgia's gesture was sublime. " Look. *All that for a shilling!* " she murmured as she rose.

X X I

Hail, hyacinth! Harbinger of spring . . ." Miss Hospice hesitated.

Before being whirled away, before descending deeper, it would be well to decide in what situation it was to be.

Should it be growing or cut. Should it be lying severed. Besmirched. Should it be placed in some poor weary hand, withering upon a quilt. Should it wave upon a hill-top, or break between the slabs of crumbling marble of the theatre tiers beneath the Acropolis; the soul of a spectator. Should it be well wired, writhing in a wreath. Or, should it be a Roman hyacinth, in which case, should she trace Christianity to its sources, musing on many a mummery by the way?

She raised a delicate witty face.

" Or . . . should she seek another flower instead? Above her the branches of the chestnut-trees rocked rhythmically. A warm wind rippling round St. Dorothy stirred the dark violet of the Bougainvillæa along the wall.

" What have you found? " Lady Anne inquired.

She was seated before the Palace, a panther skin upon her knee.

" Only——"

" Then come and help me, do. To make it less schismatical, I believe I'm going to take off the tail."

" Oh no. Give it a careless twist."

Lady Anne snapped her scissors.

" It's such an infamy! " she declared.

" Mrs. Shamefoot will say you tried to slight her if you harm a hair."

" I begin to think we've made a mistake. . . ."

" Well, she's in the saddle now. The window's up."

" I fear it'll cause a good deal of horror, scandal and surprise."

" I don't see why it should."

" It must be altogether impossible or why aren't we allowed to go near? Why must it be concealed behind a thousand towel-horses, and a million screens? Oh, Madge, you haven't a conception what I shall endure when the curtains come away. My dear, I shall probably have to sit down. All my amusement in the procession's *gone*."

And Lady Anne buried her face in her panther skin because of the sun.

" No doubt it's better than we expect. Kitty Wookie got a glimpse from the organ loft."

" She's such a cunning creature. What does she say? "

" She says it's a thing quite by itself. Apart."

" What does she mean by that? "

" She says, of course, it's entirely without reticence. . . ."

" For instance! "

" Apparently, the features are most carefully modelled. The ennui of half the world is in her eyes— almost, as always. And she is perched upon a rather bewildering throne, in a short silver tunic, showing her ankles up to her knees."

" Aurelia always said it would jar."

" It depends. Miss Wookie's easily scared. Very likely it's exquisitely lovely."

" I wouldn't willingly offend the Segry-Constables or the Nythisdenes or the Doneburning'ems or the Duke."

" I should tack a pocket to my libbard skin and let it make very little difference. . . ."

" Walter has told her she shall sleep a night in the Cathedral whenever she likes."

" He might have offered her the pink room here for the matter of that."

" It wouldn't do. She wishes to watch the colour roll back into the glass again."

" What a curious caprice! "

" I call it simply shallow."

" I'd die of terror. Mrs. Cresswell—they say, constantly . . ."

" Oh, nonsense! At most she'll confront the dark."

" For a nervous soul what could be more appalling?"

" You forget she isn't timid."

" It's hard to tell. She gave me the saddest, the whiptest, look last night as I passed her in the lane."

" Those tristful glances of hers are so irritating. Especially when everyone tries to kill her with kindness."

" That's probably why she does it."

" Well, I'd be so glad if you'd leave a book for her at the ' Four Fans ' whenever you go for a walk."

" Such an address almost makes one flurried."

" Still, poor thing, one understands intuitively, she wouldn't choose the Cresswell Arms. . . . And to stop, on the contrary, at Stockingham, where Lord Blueharnis I believe . . . And the Flagellites, of course, is overrun still by a firm from . . . And, frankly, I'm not altogether sorry. For, if there's anything I dislike, it's a house-warming."

" In Ashringford what egotists we are."

" Are we? "

" Tell me where the book is I'm to bear."

" It's here; Harvester's *Vaindreams!* "

" Not exactly the kind of book, is it, to take to her? "

" Why not? He has such a strange, peculiar style. His work calls to mind a frieze with figures of varying heights trotting all the same way. If one should by chance turn about it's usually merely to stare or to sneer or to make a grimace. Only occasionally his figures care to beckon. And they seldom really touch."

" He's too cold. Too classic, I suppose."

" Classic! In the *Encyclopædia Britannica* his style is described as *odd spelling, brilliant and vicious*."

" All the same, dear, if you wouldn't mind carrying it across."

" Shall I allude to the tail at all while I'm there? "

" Too late! I fear it's already off."

Lady Anne turned.

She was sufficiently alert to feel the vibration from a persistent pair of eyes.

" May I come in? "

With her weight entirely on one foot and an arm raised towards a gilt rosette Miss Wardle was leaning against the wrought-iron gate.

" By all means do."

" Might I have a word with the Bishop? "

" Unhappily, he's gone round to Miss Spruce."

" Something serious? "

" I trust not. She has sent to him so often *in extremis* that really——"

" Then perhaps I'd better confess to you."

Lady Anne glanced away.

Clouds, like scattered cities, dashed the blue.

" You needn't," she said. " I guess. I sympathise. Or will try to. You mean to leave us for St. John's! "

" St. John's is still without a roof."

" But ultimately, I understand, it will have one."

Miss Wardle drew a deep breath.

" No," she said, slightly shocked, " it's not that—I'm married! "

" Already! "

" I can scarcely credit it either."

" To Mr. Pet? "

" *Lippo Lippi* man! He's too sweet to be true."

" I'm delighted. I 'm glad you seem so happy."

" . . . He's twenty-three. . . . Five for elegance. Four for luck. Three for fate! "

" Of course, now, he'll need a little change? "

" A change! But Peter raves about Ashringford. He says there's nowhere like it."

" No honeymoon? "

Mrs. Pet opened a black parasol.

" Oh no," she said. " A honeymoon must always end in a certain amount of curiosity. So we've decided not to have one, but just stop here."

" It's really refreshing to find anyone nowadays who tries to avoid a fuss! "

" Peter, you see, insisted that the wedding should be quite—quite—quiet. For although you mightn't think it, he's as sensitive, in his way, as anybody in the town. And so I simply walked from Wormwood to Violet Villas with a travelling-clock and a bag."

" How dull. And surely a trifle dusty? "

" It was my first small sacrifice," Mrs. Pet said, sitting down. " As a girl I used always to say I would be married in my *point d'espagne*."

" You must make up for it at the unveiling. A dot of gold . . . against those old monks' stalls. . . ."

" I'm very uncertain yet whether I shall go."

" Indeed, I don't feel up to it myself."

" After all, one isn't always inclined for church! "

Lady Anne fetched a sigh.

" I've a tiny favour to ask," she said.

Mrs. Pet twirled, quite slightly, her parasol.

" If you wish to be really charming exert your influence! Keep your husband at home."

" I'm afraid I don't understand."

" During the little masque amuse your husband indoors."

" But I've no influence with him at all! "

" Have you none . . .? "

" Hardly any."

175

" At any rate promise to do what you can."

Mrs. Pet stared, reflective, across the *mors-in-vita* of the Cathedral green.

" I realise my limitations," she said.

" But you mustn't! "

" According to *The Ashringford Chronicle* there'll be almost a procession."

" Oh, nothing half so formal. . . ."

" And one of the Olneys, it appears, as the curtains fall away, will break from behind a pillar with a basket of orchids, and say: '*Accept these poor flowers.*' "

" Not in the Cathedral: only in the porch."

" And those foolish, silly Scouts are to fire off minute-guns from the walls."

" I haven't seen the *Chronicle*."

" Sometimes," Mrs. Pet protested, " I have no loftier wish than to look upon the world with Kate Greenaway's eyes! "

Lady Anne shivered.

"I'm all nerves," she explained, "to-day, and here's Hypolita and the Bishop! "

It was Hypolita's turn.

Aurelia had gone away to a pale silver palace in Bath, where she was casting into purest English the *Poemetti* of Pascoli.

" We looked in for a moment at the Four Fans," Dr. Pantry said.

" Well! . . ."

" Mrs. Shamefoot wasn't quite up, but I spoke to her under the door."

" Anything new? "

" She sent her love! . . . She will make her vigil on the eve of the day."

" Surely if she spends a night in the Cathedral somebody should be within call? "

" Things change so, don't they," Hypolita said,

"when the daylight goes? Frequently, even the shadow of a feather boa . . ."

" Who would look after her? "

" One of the students, perhaps——"

" Ah, no flirtations! "

" It should be an old, or *quite* an elderly man."

" What elderly person is there? "

" In this neighbourhood there're so many. There's such a choice! "

The Bishop was affected.

" I don't mind being ninety."

" You, Walter? Certainly not."

" Mr. Poyntz, perhaps. . . ."

" He'd need to raise a bed."

" Still, on Sunday he manages wonderfully well without."

" I'm down in the garden every morning by five . . ."

" My dear, what ever for? "

" Besides, she refuses! She desires to be alone."

Lady Anne gazed at her sister-in-law in dismay.

How was it possible that one did nothing to such a terribly shiny nose?

She considered it etched against the effortless chain of hills, designed, apparently, to explain that the world was once made in a week.

The morning was so clear the distances seemed to shrink away—one could even trace the racecourse, to its frail pavilion, by the artificial fence.

" It will be so nice when it's all over," she exclaimed.

" All over, Anne? "

" The unveiling——"

" Life was never meant to be quite easy! "

When Hypolita began upon *Life* she simply never stopped.

Dr. Pantry raised his wife's wrist and examined the watch.

" Are you coming, my dear, to——? "
" Oh, my dear, very likely! "
" Then make haste: the bells will begin directly. . . ."
But to-day she invented an entirely new excuse.
" I must run indoors *first* to wave my white hairs,"
she said.

XXII

A SMART, plain sky stretched starless above St. Dorothy. The night was sultry, sweet and scented.

Miss Thumbler shrugged her pretty, crippled shoulders and pressed volcanically her hands.

" Beautiful! " she murmured. " But how walled in! "

" Answer me! " he said.

" Oh, George . . . haven't I enough already? Of course I cannot recall all the trifling ins and outs. Although, I believe, he kissed me, once, in the Vermeer Room at the National Gallery! "

She turned away.

These continual jealous scenes. . . .

Only a few hours back there had been an aria from *Tosca*, in St. John's.

There came a babel of voices.

On the lawn and in the lighted loggia the total town was waiting for Mrs. Shamefoot to pass. And as usual everyone was turning on the hose.

" . . . Vanna! Mrs. Nythesedene got a palm there . . . ages ago. She said . . she could see her . . . plainly . . . in the little room behind the shop . . . tearing the white lilac out of a wreath . . . and wiring it up for . . ."

" Her dull white face seems to have no connection with her chestnut hair! "

" . . . with *him* to Palestine last spring. Oh, dear me, I thought I should have died at Joppa! "

" You mix them with olives and a drop of cognac."

" What could be more tiresome than a wife that bleats? "

179

" His denunciations of the Government nearly brought the lustres down."

" I can't get him to come with me. He doesn't like the pendant lamps."

". . . above-board, when one can! "

". . . Half the profits."

" Ce gros Monsignor Parr! "

". . . A day together."

". . . Rabbits."

". . . As tall as Iss'y."

". . . Precedence! "

". . . A regular peruke."

". . . An interesting trio! "

" A tiara swamps her."

" She will become florid in time. Just like her mother."

" Don't! "

" For him a *tête-à-tête* would be a *viva voce*. . . ."

". . . glare."

". . . lonely! "

". . . no sympathy for——"

". . . Idolatry."

". . . a top! "

" I heard a noise. A sound. But country servants are so rough. Aren't they? Breaking, dropping, chipping things. I've scarcely a dish that isn't cracked. . . ."

". . . escape! "

". . . *is* such a duck in his . . ."

" The only genuine one was Jane."

". . . poison."

". . . fuss. . . ."

" My husband was always shy. He is shy of everybody. He even runs away from me! "

" Let us sell the house, dear," she said, " but keep the car! We can drive round and round the park in it at night. And it looks so charming for the day."

Lady Anne trailed slowly up and down. She seemed worn-out.

"I'll go on," Hypolita said. "Life's too short to walk so slow."

"As you please. But there's no escape from Eternity," Mr. Pet's voice came, unexpectedly booming out.

At which vision, of continual middle age, the younger Miss Flowerman fainted.

On a litter, in the garden, where the stairs streamed up towards the house, Miss Spruce surveyed the scene with watchful, wondering eyes. It was cruel to be an invalid with her energetic mind. . . .

Still, a good deal came her way.

"Come now, and meet him, and get it over!" Mrs. Henedge was exhorting Winsome Brookes.

It was her first appearance anywhere since the change.

Attended by George Calvally, Mira Thumbler, Winsome and Monsignor Parr, she would have responded willingly to an attack.

From beneath a black bandeau sparkling with brilliants and an aigrette breaking several ways she seemed to Miss Spruce like some radiant Queen of Night.

"Anybody born in 1855 I've no desire to meet," Winsome declared.

"Hush! Remember your *future!*" the relentless woman murmured, dragging him towards Lord Brassknocker to be introduced.

". . . Belongs to the Junior Carlton, the Arts, and to several night *cabarets.*"

"Sir Caper Frisk was explaining to me that cocktails——"

By the great gold gates that closed at dusk the choir was waiting to give three cheers.

"Poor mites! I hear they've been told to give four," Mrs. Wookie said.

" What are we waiting for? "

" I haven't a notion."

" The moon——"

" It must have been the year that Drowsy-Dreamy-Dora won the Derby. . . ."

" The old Duke begins to look a bit hipped."

" One tooth missing. And only half rouged. On one side only. I'd not call her pretty."

" Pan? "

" . . . descended from *a waiter.*"

" If anything takes him to town it's the cattle-show."

" I loathe London."

" ' Sable, sable, indeed ! ' I said. There's no depth to the skin. Nothing to fathom. It might be crocodiles."

Monsignor Parr drew in his feet. He had been so very nearly asleep. All his life he had waited for something attractive to happen. Usually, now, he would sit huddled up like a Canopic jar saying nothing at all.

" . . . too tired to make converts. . . ."

" . . . totter from party to party. . . ."

" How do you do? "

" . . . sorry."

" If my father marries again it will be to some sweet soul to stir the fire."

" . . . does enjoy a rubber! "

" The lanes round Dawn are so narrow. And Sir Sirly and Lady James. . . . Well, there's hardly room for us all. . . . "

" Only Miss Knowle and Mrs. Lloyd! "

" . . . sheet-lightning? "

" Naturally, for the moment," Mrs. Shamefoot was confessing, " it's the least bit gorgeous, perhaps. But one has to look ahead. Posterity? "

" Such a pity not to have gone halves. You and Lady Castleyard together. A Beaumont-and-Fletcher ——"

" So, actually, you've come! "

182

" What a wonderful wrap. My dear, what skins! "

" In case you should feel faint at all in the night you'll find a lobster mayonnaise and some champagne in the vestry! "

" Dear Lady Anne, how could you dream of such a thing? "

" In the grey of dawn, when a thousand grinning fiends peer down on you, you may be very glad of a little something. . . ."

Above the toppling timber, and the long low vineries, towered St. Dorothy. Urging each quivering leaf, and every blade of grass, to strain higher, *higher*.

" I hope you've a nice warm pair of stockings? " Mrs. Wookie wailed.

Mrs. Shamefoot stretched wearily above her head some starry spangled stuff.

" The mornings," she observed, " are still quite chilly! "

" I'm looking everywhere for Kate. It's like searching for a needle in a bundle of hay."

" It ought not to be! "

" You'll find Miss Wookie in the drawing-room, playing Siegfried's Journey."

" I must make sure she's ordered our *fly*."

" A representative of the *Chronicle* would so much like to know——"

" Not now. Just when my spirit cries to be alone everything that's earthly seems to pass between! "

" He merely desires to ask you how you are."

" How I am? "

" How you feel."

" I feel such a strange sadness. You might tell him." She moved away.

Miss Thumbler had apparently consented to dance.

Stiffening her fingers and thrusting out her chin, she began slightly to sway, as though pursuing an invisible ideal.

" Sartorious always said she had a horrid mind! "
" I'm delighted she's so busy."
" Really——"
" She's been doing her utmost to *will* the tower down upon us this last half-hour."
" You mean——"
" I'm afraid so."
" Could anyone be so rough? "
"No, I haven't yet finished," Miss Valley was saying. "Alas, a little fame! One buys it at such a price. . . ."
Beneath the big blue Persia-tree, the Miss Chalfonts lay quite still. They had attained their calm.
" It might be almost the Hesperides! " Lady Georgia declared.
" . . . foot's on the wane! "
" In a gloomy corner she is still quite pretty."
Mrs. Shamefoot held up her fan.
" . . . the crops! "
" Ah, here comes our dreadsome friend! "
" Leave him to me," Miss Valley said. " I'll undertake to tame him."
" Use some of your long writing words to him, my dear! "
" Shall I? Would you like me to? "
" Few people are worth untidying one's hair for," Winsome Brookes observed.
" Mrs. Shamefoot! "
" Yes, my angel."
Master Guy Fox was staring at her with great googoo eyes like a morning in May.
" Mr. Pet says you've done something to be ashamed of."
" I? . . Oh, good heavens! " Mrs. Shamefoot began to laugh.
" We've such trouble," his mother said, " to get him to close his mouth. He gapes. But at Eton, probably, there are instructors who will attend to *that*."

" There are certain to be classes——"

" Perhaps even oftener than any other! "

And the Dean smiled sheepishly and tried to look less like a wolf. It was a favourite expression of his when addressing youth.

" What would you like to do eventually if you live to be a man? "

Almost nervously St. Dorothy chimed the hour.

" I would like to hang in a large gold bird-cage in the window."

" Is that all? "

" And be a bird! "

" And not a wild one? "

" Supported? "

" Kept! "

" Oh, you lazy little thing."

" I wish my boy had his quiet tastes," the Duchess said. " A child in the Life Guards runs away with so much money! "

" O-o-o-h. . . . When that Miss Thumbler bends so far it makes me quite afraid."

" I long to see La Taxeira in a new set of attitudes."

" Has she fresh ones? "

" Oh, she's unearthly! "

" They say she never dances without her Pompeian pavement! "

" Dear Lady Barrow, I've had no opportunity before! . . . We seem, now, surrounded by water as we are . . . quite to be floating. The Castle is my *yacht*."

" I do so love a wreck."

" From our upper stories, I must tell you, the Asz has almost a look of the sea! One has an impression of chestnut-trees and swans, and perfectly pink roses."

" Some day, perhaps——"

" Unfortunately from my room, sir, there is really nothing to admire. . . . A view over tiresome chimney pots. And that is all."

" I adore tiresome chimney pots."

" Where is everybody going? "

" Indoors. There's such an absorbing . . ."

Through the wide windows of the drawing-room someone could be heard to say:

" Town Eclogues! . . . Epistle from Arthur Grey the Footman. Words by Lady Mary Wortley. Music by Chab-bon-nière."

" Delightful! "

" So suitable! "

" Ingenious! "

" Ingeniousness *is* so rare! "

" And so enchanting! "

" Prevent the Pets——"

" Dear Peter," Mrs. Pet murmured, tapping her husband lightly, " he is everything I admire, and like and love."

" I wonder I'm not in strong hysterics," Lady Anne confessed.

" Before the Monsignor wakes wouldn't it be well to uncover the piano? "

" Uncover it? . . ."

" Remove that cope! "

" How can I, while——"

A. G. declared:

" ' Though bid to go, I quite forgot to move;
  You know not that stupidity was love! ' "

" Afterwards, then! . . ."

" You have the sweetest heart! "

" Should you hear the organ sounding in the night," Mrs. Shamefoot remarked, " you'll realise it's *me*."

" How piqued! "

" An over-sensitive person in the country is always a strain."

" Try."

" Oh, I'm sure I never could——"

" I should never, never, no never, have believed it to be so difficult to enlist a *prima donna*."

" Flatterer! "

" You wouldn't fail us! "

" My poor repertoire," Mrs. Henedge explained. " If I sing anything now it's *Divinités du Styx*."

" Gluck! "

" Jeanne Grannier *en vacances* couldn't equal her! " Lady Georgia affirmed.

Up the steps, from the garden, clitter-clatter, with the agility of an antelope, came Mrs. Budd, whose claim to being the oldest woman in Ashringford nobody seemed likely to dispute.

The piano had lured her from beneath the shadow of the trees. She stood mumbling and blinking in the light, leaning on the arm of Reggie Cresswell of the choir.

" Her son is sexton here! "

Mrs. Shamefoot held out a hand.

" I'm so happy——"

" Here, Reggie," Winsome said.

" Oh, what a darling! "

" We want him to sing."

" Sing? "

" *Come away Death*, or something."

" Shakespeare is all very well in his way—and in his place."

Reggie looked shy.

" He's been crying! "

" Tears! "

" What is the matter? "

" Mr. Pet——"

" What did he do, dear? "

" I aroused his provocation."

" You aroused his . . . that surely was very indiscreet."

" Yes, miss."

" Reggie's all feelings. Aren't you, Reggie? "

" Yes, miss."

" Reggie will do anything for sixpence," Mrs. Budd said. " He is a true Cresswell."

" She introduced the parlour or salon," Miss Valley observed. " She helped, too, to give afternoon-tea its vogue: the French five o'clock. She was also one of our original vegetarians. Oh, my dear, she took the silliest things. Her adoration for apricots is well known. She would tin them. And sometimes she would sleep for days on days together——"

" So sensible."

" And her love for animals! Even as a girl she would say: ' And I shall have a doll and a bird and talk to it.' "

" Why not them? "

" Because she prefers a solecism! And then, her fondness for flowers. . . . ' How beautiful violets are,' she says, ' in a room, just as the day is closing. I know of no other flower *quite* so intense.' "

" There's a sensuousness, a concreteness in her ideas. Isn't there? "

" She was so human. So practical. An artist in the finest sense."

" You'll quite miss her when you've done."

" I dare say I shall."

" And afterwards who will take her place? "

" I've scarcely settled yet. I never care to arrange anything at all ahead. I dislike a definite programme. Perhaps, a Judas Iscariot——"

" ' Vapours of Vanity and strong champagne,' " Arthur was beginning to drawl.

Mrs. Shamefoot glanced about her.

The moon shone out now high above the trees. In smoke-like, dreamy spirals streamed the elms, breaking towards their zeniths into incredible *ich diens*.

" Between us all," the Bishop said, " I was afraid we should lose the key! "

She took it, seizing it slightly.

There were ribands attached, countless streaming strings.

" How charming! "

" It has been circulating about like one of those romances of Mrs.——"

" Am I to lead the way? "

" A coterie of ladies, first, expect a little prayer."

" A prayer! "

" Lady Victoria Webster Smith insists on something of the kind."

" You know she has never really got over her *mésalliance.* . . ."

" What am I to do? "

Mrs. Shamefoot raised her face.

Above her, silver-white, a rose dangled deep asleep.

" There's one thing I've done," she said, " I've sent to the Inn for a hat."

" Indeed! "

" One feels securer, somehow, beneath a few fierce feathers."

" You're not afraid."

" Certainly not."

" Permit me to say you look bewitching."

" This unfinished rag——"

" Has teased——"

" When she comes it will be as if a Doge espoused the Adriatic! "

" Hark . . . to your soulless flock! . . ."

" In Ashringford, if souls are rare, we've at least some healthy spirits."

" Dear Dr. Pantry, everybody's wondering where you are! "

" You seem upset."

" Lady Anne is over-tired, I fear. These warm airless nights. . . . Just as Miss Pontypool was commencing her second encore——"

Mrs. Shamefoot slipped away.

In the garden all was dim.

Along a walk laced with weeping violet fuchsias she skimmed, glancing apprehensively from side to side.

There appeared to be a good deal going on.

In the chiaroscuro of the shrubberies marriages were being arranged. . . .

On a garden bench in a shower of moonlight an Ashringford matron was comparing shadows with her child.

" And why *not*, pray? " she seemed to ask.

" Marry. . . . Have a substantial husband? Oh no, I couldn't, I couldn't, I really couldn't."

" Well, dear, there's no need to get so agitated. It wouldn't be—just yet."

Round and round a great gloomy bush of thorn Miss Thumbler was circling in the oblivion of a dance, while, threading here and there, Lady Barrow annulled a thousand awkward calls. . . . " Your poor husband." " Your interesting son." " Your gifted girl." " Your delightful wife."

Observing her the Miss Chalfonts were assailed again. Monsignor Parr, revealing his mind, moved a finger from forehead to chin, and from ear to ear. And through the gilded gates that closed at dusk Mrs. Henedge's dog had found a way and was questing inscrutably about. . . .

" He ought to be muzzled! " Mrs. Wookie declared.

" Come now. Just once more! " Mrs. Henedge was entreating still.

" But I'm so tired," Winsome said, " of meeting other people. I want other people to meet me."

" Really, and what should you say to them? "

" Nothing; I don't know."

Mrs. Shamefoot hurried on.

A dark cloud like an immense wild bird had drifted across the moon.

Were the gods, she wondered, taking any interest in her affair?

" Oh, don't spoil it," someone she did not recognise implored. "*I think Alice and Dick are holy.* They're each eighteen. And they're in love! . . ."

Mrs. Shamefoot turned aside.

Before her, serene, soared St. Dorothy.

It was a joy to admire such beautifully balanced towers.

" No, I never once lost hope! " she informed a grimacing, ghoulish gargoyle of a sprite.

Those demons, imps, fiends and fairies with horns like stalactites and indignant, scurrying angels and virgins trampling horrors beneath their firm, mysterious feet, and the winged lion of Mark and the winged ox of Luke and the rows and tiers of things enskied above the cavernous deep doors were *part of her escort now!*

And within, elusive, brittle, responsive to every mood, in every minute, and every year improving. . . .

" Shall we go? "

" Certainly. Let's."

Figures flitted by.

She bolted in.

The utter void unnerved her.

" A collier," she reflected, " would laugh at me. He would say . . . He would *call it light!* . . ."

She sank across a chair.

In the dark nothingness the flags drooped fearfully. . . .

Imaginatively, she strove to hold her man.

" Bill? "

" She admired his full lips, his tip-tilted, inquisitive nose. She thought he had a soft Italian face. . . ."

Marble quarries!

Dirty, disgusting coal!

She recalled visiting marble quarries. Soco and she together. " Oh dear! . . . That slow sad drive. Up, and up, and up! And when the road turned, such a surprising view. . . . Then the coachman invited somebody on to the box . . . I remember I said nothing! "

" A footstool! "

She lay back on her chair . . . relieved.

How still it was. . . . She could almost hear the worms nibbling the carved images of the saints!

" My poor maid must be searching everywhere for me in vain. . . ."

Which little hat would she bring? Lately, she had become so revoltingly stupid. . . . What had come over her at all? She was so changed. . . .

She could make out the Ashringford Juliet now borne as though a leaf on a misty-shadow sea. And, more massive, the Blueharnis monument of course! Over the canopy crouched an occult, outrageous thing, phosphorescent in places. Beyond, an old statesman was reclining, his head resting upon a confused heap of facts.

He had a look of Soco.

Where would he be while she was vigiling here? The club. . . . Savoy. . . .

Never in her life had she thought so much about him before. Twice in two minutes!

That pretty Miss Chance. . . .

Oh, well! . . .

And in future, this was to be her home!

Had she chosen wisely? . . . By waiting, perhaps——

Cupolas and minarets whizzed and whirled.

After all, Overcares had its points. . . . It rose with brilliance from its hill. It made a deep impression from the train. One dropped one's paper, one changed

one's place, chatter hung suspended in the air. . . .
Dear Dorothy was in a hollow rather. The trees
shaded it so. Sintrap, too, had style. And Mawling.
. . . But, there, there was nothing to regret. Placed
in the midst of the town. Stifled! All about it stood
such fussy, frightful shops. Post-cards, bibelots, toys
for tourists. . . . And a cab-stand and a horse-trough
and a pension. And, besides, the stone was changing
yellow—almost as if it had jaundice. And Mrs.
Whooper had said . . .

Did such trifles matter now?

To be irrelevant at such a minute. . . .

At the Inn to-night she had thought ten thousand
thrilling things were taking place about her.

How long ago that seemed!

She had spent the day at the Flagellites in a corner
of the orchard listening to the ecstasy of the bees.
And then Pacca had come to rouse her. And she had
returned to the Inn through the cornfields by the Asz.
How clear the river ran! Every few yards she had
paused to stand entranced. And a young man with a
fishing-rod and in faint mourning had entreated her
earnestly not. " I could not watch you do it," he had
said. " Not that you would spoil my . . . At least! "
And his hands were quite hot and clammy. " What
is a flaw more or less in an imperfect world? " he had
asked. And he had accompanied her back to the Inn.
And she had wept a little while she dressed. . . .
And a white-winged moth had fluttered into the lamp.
And she had gone to close the window. And everywhere the stars had sprung out like castanets and then
gone in again. And the sunset had been heroic.

And she had waited so anxiously for to-night!

Mortifications had paved the way to it.

Was it only to suffer aridity and disappointment?

Such emotions were experienced best at home.

And would vignettes give way to visions?

Bill again.

" No, no! "

Or Satan. . . .

With dismay she waved her fan.

She was aware once more of leering lips. A tip-
tilted, inquisitive nose. . . .

" Then the coachman," she began, speaking in her
agony aloud, " invited somebody on to the box. I
remember I said nothing——"

XXIII

EVER since Mr. Calvally had taken a total adieu of his wife the building operations in Ashringford had practically ceased.

" It is certainly unfortunate," Mrs. Henedge complained, " that the daughter of my architect should run away with my painter—the husband, too, of my most valued friend! "

She was in town again, for someone, of course, must be brought to finish the frescoes at St. John's.

" If only I were able," she declared, " I would finish them myself! "

For, after all, what was there, when one came to consider?

A torso . . . an arm of a centurion . . . a bit of breast-plate . . . a lady—*if any lady* . . . a few haloes . . . and a page.

Carefully she arranged the items in a list while waiting for the *School of Calvally*, Andrew who had failed to come.

From her writing-table, whenever she looked up, she caught the reflection of her car in the downstairs windows of the house opposite.

" When I invited him to my fireside," she reflected, " no doubt he thought it was to roast him. But I was in such a tremor, I hardly remember what I said. I might have been bespeaking paste pearls——"

And she recalled the casual words of the master.

" Andrew can't draw," he had often said; " he gets into difficulties and he begins to trill! "

And on another occasion he had remarked: " All his work is so pitch dark—that little master of the pitch dark. . . ." And had not she too foolishly mistaken his *Ecce Homo* loaned about at pre-impressionist shows for an outing of Charles I?

And here was she sitting waiting for him?

"Poor Mary," she reflected. "I ought to have gone round to her before. Though, when I do . . . she is sure to set upon me! She will say I threw them together."

And, perplexed, she picked up a pen, a paper-knife, a letter-weight——

A postscript from Lady Twyford peeped at her.

"In recommending to you Martin as chauffeur," she read, "I feel I should say that his corners are terribly *tout juste*."

What could be better in her present mood? She would have preferred to fly.

"I adore an aeroplane," she breathed; "it gives one such a tint——"

She rang.

"Thérèse? *My things!*"

"Oh, London. Native place! Oh, second string to my bow! Oh, London dear!" she prayed.

Whose uplifting was it?

As Martin sped along she was moved.

"The way the trees lean . . . the way the branches grow——" she addressed the park.

How often, as a child, had she sat beneath them, when, with hands joined primly across her solar plexus, the capital, according to nurse, was just a big wood—with some houses in it.

She found Mrs. Calvally propped up by a pink pillow shelling peas.

It brought to mind her husband's disgraceful defence.

"How could I ever have been happy with her," he had asked, "when her favourite colour is crushed strawberry?"

"I had no idea," Mrs. Calvally said, "that you were in town."

"I felt I could not pass——"

"Everyone has been so good to us."

"Yesterday," Raphael said, who was lying upon the floor, "a cat, a peacock-person, an old lion and a butterfly all came to inquire. And to-day, such an enormous, big, large, huge, terrific——"

"Yesterday, dear, will do."

Mrs. Henedge raised an eyebrow.

"I was afraid," she said, "I should find you in one of Lucile's black dreams——"

"Tell me all your news!"

"In the country what news is there ever? This year we fear an epidemic of yellow flowers will spoil the hay. . . ."

"I am sure the country must be quite a sight."

". . . I prefer my garden to everything in the world."

"There is a rumour that it has inspired an opera!"

"I fancy only a consecration. Mr. Brookes is certainly to be Rose. A Christmas one! He makes his début this winter."

"And *the other*, when is that to be?"

"One can only conjecture. . . . It occurred to me that very likely Andrew——"

"Oh, Andrew! An-drew can't draw. He never drew anything yet."

"Run away, dear; do."

"Besides, he's going to Deauville to decorate *a Bar.* . . . Scenes of English Life——"

"My dear, all Europe is very much alike!"

"And all the world, for the matter of that."

"I heard from George this morning."

"Really, what does he say?"

"Oh, it's only a line. So formal, with the *date*, and everything. And there is a tiny message, too, from her."

" Poor demoniac——"

" Of course I haven't seen you since! "

" No——"

Mrs. Calvally settled her pillows.

" She came round like a whirlwind," she began.

" . . . Manner means so much."

" A tornado. I was just putting on my *shawl*. You know how he loved anything strange——"

" Well! "

Mrs. Calvally paused.

" I think there must be thunder about," she said.

" I've been at the point of death all day."

" And where are they now? "

" In Italy. Trailing about. And he went away with such an overweight of luggage. . . ."

" I expect he took his easels! "

" This morning the letter was from Rimini. It appears it reminds them of Bexhill. . . . And the hotel, it seems, so noisy."

" How painfully dull it sounds."

" Quite uninteresting! "

" I think it sounds jolly."

" Shall we evoke Morocco with a rose and lilac shoe? "

" What would be the good of that? "

" No good at all, my treasure, only it might be fun."

Mrs. Henedge struggled to her feet.

" Evoke Morocco! " she said. " I fear I haven't time. I've a dentist and a palmist, and——"

She surveyed half nervously the shoe.

There was hardly any rose and scarcely any lilac. It was *a crushed strawberry*.

XXIV

" To-day I'll have threepennyworth! "

In a flowing gown tinged with melancholy and a soupçon rouged Mrs. Shamefoot stood ethereal at her gate.

She laughed lightly.

" And, perhaps, I'll have some cream. . . ."

With the movement of a priestess she handed him a jar.

" That jar," she said, " belonged, once, to . . . So mind it doesn't break."

And while the lad ladled she studied with insouciance the tops of the chimneys across the way.

The sky was full of little birds. Just at her gate a sycamore-tree seemed to have an occult fascination of its own.

Whole troops of birds would congregate there, flattening down each twig and spray, perpetually outpouring.

" Before I came here," she inquired, " were the birds so many? "

He shook his head.

" There was only an owl."

" It's extraordinary."

" Shall I book the cream? "

" What is the matter with the bells? "

" They're sounding for the Sisters."

" Are they ill? Again? "

" They died last night—of laughter."

" What amused them, do you know? "

" They were on the golf links. . . ."

" Death, sometimes, is really a remedy."

" Soon there'll be no call for a dairy. What with the river——"

" Indeed it's more like somewhere in *Norway* now! "

" Not that, in milk——"

" Crazes change so, don't they? "

" A nice deep pail of——"

" Since yesterday, has anyone else? . . . "

" It's a pretty jar," he said in a subdued voice. " What is it? "

" That's Saxe," she said, as she carefully closed the door.

The long flaying room was flooded by the evening sun.

" One needs an awning," she murmured, setting down the cream.

Before the house stretched a strip of faint blue sand. There were times when it brought to mind the Asz.

Only last night she had trailed towards the window, and with the tip of her toe . . .

She turned, half charmed, away. There could still be seen the trace . . .

" I think the house will be the greatest success! "

Of course, the walls were rather carpeted with pictures——

There was the *Primitive*, that made the room, somehow, seem so calm. And a *Blessed Damozel*—that fat white thing. And a Giorgione, so silky and sweet. And a Parma angel. And the " study-of-me-which-is-*such*-an-infamy! "

" I must have blinds," she exclaimed.

It was tiresome there were none now since Georgia was coming in to tea.

How prim the cups were upon their china tray!

She had placed them there herself. . . .

In a bowl beside them floated a few green daisies with heavy citron hearts.

And if they chose to make eyes at the cherries, what did it matter, since the background was so plain?

She glanced at her reflection.

" O mon miroir, rassure-moi; dis moi que je suis belle, qui je serai belle éternellement! "

She paused, causelessly sad.

Even here, the world, why . . . one was still in it——

" We should pray for those who do not comprehend us! " she murmured. And, of course, that would end in having a chaplain. Or begin by having one.

A camera study of her sister, Mrs. Roy Richards, a woman whose whims would have made the theme of a book, or a comedy *en famille*, with her seven children standing round her nearly naked, had arrived, only lately, as if to recall her to herself.

" Not since the last famine . . . " she murmured, tucking it into a drawer.

" Ah, there! " One could hardly mistake that horn.

. . .

She lifted the wooden pin in the door and peered through the grill.

" Who knocks? "

" A sinner."

" A couple," Lady Castleyard corrected, " of the very worst. Regular devils."

" Come in. Unfortunately, my Gretchen has gone out."

" I hear you are achieving sainthood by leaps and bounds! "

Mrs. Shamefoot embraced her guests.

" I fear . . . it's far more gradual."

" It must be so desolate for you, dear, here all alone, cut off from everybody."

" I love my solitude."

" What ever do you find to do, in the long evenings? "

" I'm studying Dante——"

Lady Georgia rolled her eyes.

" I imagine you keep a parakeet," she said. " Where is it? "

Mrs. Shamefoot busied herself with the tea.

" Have you noticed the birds? " she asked. " Such battalions. . . . And before I came there was only an owl! "

" I admire your garden. Those tragic thickets of thorns——"

" I think the autumn here should be simply sublime."

" I will witness it, I hope, from my roof-top! I'm like an Oriental when I get up there. I'm sure I was one, once."

" How, dear? "

" Oh, don't expect me to explain."

" Jack would insist still that you had saved the country."

" Locally, of course."

" He's so enchanted with the window. He has got me to change our pew. ' Poor Biddy,' he said to me, ' she looks really royal. A kind of grandeur——' "

" Several young men in town seem struck by it too. They like to sit before it. I believe they even kneel. . . . So annoying! Often, just when I want to be there myself——"

" I'm glad you go somewhere. It's wrong to withdraw yourself too completely. Without a servant even! "

" My servant, Gretchen, ran, silly child, to the post office about a week ago."

" I wonder you let her. . . ."

" I needed stamps."

" Stamps! "

" Soco had scribbled. . . ."

" What are his views? "

202

" He speaks of a visit. He has never seen St. Dorothy. I received such a volume from him this morning, quires and quires and quires, all about nothing."

" You must bring him to Stockingham when he comes. We're giving *The Playboy of the Western World* in the Greek Theatre. . . . I don't know how it will be!"

" Julia's Pegeen——"

" I see she's reviving *Magda.*"

" So she is. But you know nothing lasts her long."

" And her strange maid, apparently, is going on the stage. She is to take a part of a duchess."

Lady Castleyard yawned.

" I love your room," she said. " It's so uncommon."

" I want to show you my mourner's lamps."

" Where are they?"

" In my bedroom."

" Your bedroom, Biddy. I expect it's only a cell."

" It overlooks the grave-ground."

" Oh, how unpleasant!"

" I don't mind it. I like to sit in the window and watch the moon rise until the brass weather-cock on the belfry turns slowly silver above the trees . . . or, in the early dawn, perhaps, when it rains, and the whole world seems so melancholy and desolate and personal and quite intensely sad—and life an utter hoax——"

Lady Georgia rubbed away a tear.

" I don't know!" she said.

" A hoax! You wonder I can isolate myself so completely. Dear Georgia, just because I want so much, it's extraordinary how little I require."

" Don't the neighbours tire you?"

" I hardly ever see them! I am afraid I frighten Lady Anne. . . . Old Mrs. Wookie made me some advances with a *face-cloth* she had worked me for my demise. . . . And I've become quite friendly with the Pets. He has such character. Force. I am leaving him a lock of my hair."

" S-s-sh! How morbid! Shall we explore the cell? I've never seen one yet."

" I'd sooner not be over-chastened," Lady Castle-yard confessed. " It might spoil me for the antiquarians. . . . And the last time I was here I unearthed such a sweet old chair with hoofs."

" Poor Mrs. Frobisher found four Boucher panels there once."

" I'm quite sure it was once! "

Mrs. Shamefoot slid aside some folding doors.

Ashringford, all towers, turrets, walls, spires, steeples and slanting silver slates, stretched before her in the evening sun.

" I'll come as far as St. Dorothy with you," she murmured, " if you like. It's just the time I go for my quiet half-hour."

www.ingramcontent.com/pod-product-compliance
Lightning Source LLC
LaVergne TN
LVHW051026120425
808479LV00007B/248